MOUNTAIN MAN RETURNS

MOUNTAIN MAN BOOTS

A WESTERN ADVENTURE

GENE TURNEY

Copyright © 2023 by Gene Turney

Published by DS Productions

ISBN: 9798390253458

This novel, as are all my novels and everything I do, is dedicated to Cheryl, my children, grandchildren, nieces, nephews, cousin Pat, other in-laws and outlaws, and many friends' encouragements. Without the faith and encouragement of so many, this book would not exist. With great appreciation, I acknowledge the people who have provided invaluable assistance to the development of this particular novel.

FOREWORD

There comes a time when a mountain man must return to the mountains. Ears are hurting from all the noise, and it seems every day is a shootout or fistfight. Mountain Man Boots is determined to leave some of that behind. He doesn't look for trouble, but trouble seems to have a way of finding the legendary mountain man. He discovers a twelve-year-old girl named Adaline can communicate with horses and other animals as well. One such animal helps Adaline through a difficult time before Boots arrives. When he does arrive, the fight is one because Boots does not hold with those who intend to harm children.

1

Eating at the Flapjack café is one of Boots Mc Cray's favorite things to do. The café became a natural location next to the trading post. A cook, who went by the name Old Cookie, of course, hopped off a wagon train to start the café in a tent. Old Cookie prepared meals for cowboys on cattle drives. He loved doing it, but the travel began to tell on his old bones. He ran the Flapjack Café just as he ran the chuck wagon on the trail drives. The menu started out being the same, but Old Cookie expanded the selections. His help in the kitchen came from a Cheyenne woman who decided Cookie was responsible for hanging the moon. The name Toma meant the sun in her tribe, and Toma sure brought radiant sunshine to Old Cookie and the Flapjack Café.

Boots sat at his favorite table in the back of the building, close to the kitchen door. Most days, the door got propped open and he could watch Cookie and Toma working as a team. Occasionally, Toma would grab a handful of Cookie's rear end causing him to jump. Cookie never mastered the relationship part of women. That did not matter one bit to Toma. He told her he did not understand those sorts of things. Toma told him that would be just fine, she would take care of that as well and she did. Toma made Old Cookie happier than he had ever been in his sixty-seven years of life. Nobody knew Toma's age, and they were afraid to ask. While her face and her body looked to be very young, Toma told people she was not as old as Cookie, but she could catch up pretty quickly.

Those kinds of things brought a smile to the face of Boots. He earned the reputation of a legendary mountain man. He lived on the mountain and he enjoyed every minute of it. Boots brought his family to this place. He pulled his mother out of their old farm after his Cheyenne wife got her through her near-death sickness. His two sisters and brother were close to starving when Boots arrived. The man of the house left his family to fend for themselves, and they did for a while, but when their mother fell ill, everything went downhill. The little community would no longer help. Their services were stretched to the limit. The family owed the doctor, and he would no longer see to Mary's sickness. The family looked as though they were on death's door. Boots and his wife

Migisi arrived during one of the worst snow storms anyone could remember.

The fireplace in the old homestead house sat cold with no wood. The two girls and the boy were huddled together wrapped in blankets to try to keep warm. Migisi went to work to heal Mary. She suffered from a terrible case of pneumonia, and that happened to be something Migisi knew a lot about. As the daughter of Chief Ehane, her mother saw to it Migisi learned the healing skills of their tribe. In an hour, Boots cut enough firewood to get the warmth started in the house. He went to the store to buy supplies to fill the empty shelves in the kitchen. He learned the family did not possess a good reputation in the community due to the fact his father killed the blacksmith. Boots made his mind up to get his family out of the squalor. He planned to take them to a place where he felt more at home.

Mary recovered and Boots sold the farm to a neighbor. He rode his horse alongside the wagon where Mary, June, Julie, and August rode. Migisi drove the four horses Boots purchased from the man buying the farm. His thoughts began to clear and he looked forward to having his family nearby. Mary settled on the nickname Boots. His real name happened to be July. The family thought it a good idea to name their children after the name of the month when they were born. Boots of course came in July. His sister in June and the younger sister came in July, but since Boots already owned that name, they named her Julie. And then came August. Mary always teased August that had he been born a little later, his name would be September. That idea never sat well with August.

The family landed at a trading post near where the fur trapper's rendezvous was held. Those did not happen anymore because the fur trade ended. However, the trading post served as a way station for wagon trains traveling west, and occasionally east. Those travelers following the wagon train trail also stopped at the trading post. With so much traffic traveling the path, Old Cookie saw it as a natural place to hang out his café sign. He called the place the Flapjack Café because his flapjacks were known far and wide. Eventually, the track in front of the café and trading post became known as Flapjack Street.

Young August worked for the blacksmith back home, and when the first wagon train stopped at the trading post, he saw a need for a blacksmith shop. In short order, the shop got built with a corral and livery to house the four-legged animals.

Mary took over the operations at the Trading Post, and when the owner died, she became one of the first females to own a trading post. The reputation of the business stood very well. The building construction consisted of logs from the trees on the mountain. The rough-hewn board made for a nice floor as the building stood several feet off the ground. The trading post set itself apart from the most common trading posts which were lean to structures or dugouts. Those establishments also served beer and whiskey for revenue. Mary kept a firm hand to stop that kind of trade in her store.

Kit Carson sashayed through the area during a gold rush promotion prompting the construction of the Kit Carson Hotel. Rooms were few but well cared for. A lobby greeted the guests as they turned to the counter to register. Surprisingly the hotel rooms were occupied most of the time. When a wagon train rolled up to a stop, travelers would give up sleeping with the wagon for a night of comfort in a bed. The ladies also preferred that night and a meal they did not have to cook as they enjoyed the fair in the Flapjack Café.

Johnny Ross and his wife Sara owned and operated the Kit Carson Hotel. Their twelve-year-old daughter helped with the chores of keeping the rooms fresh and clean and sweeping the floors. Johnny liked to take his breakfast at the Flapjack to allow Sara to sleep a little longer. He knew that without Sara, he would be in trouble in the hotel business.

Johnny admired and respected Boots McCray. He knew of the legend and lore around the mountain man. On this day, he thought he would sit with Boots and have breakfast.

"Mind if I join you for breakfast?" Johnny asked.

Boots knew Johnny and Sara and thought well of them. He appreciated those who put in their hard work and he thought they did an admirable job raising little Adaline. Adaline had the look of her mother. Her eyes were deep brown as was her hair. The girl seemed quiet in her manner and used respectful manners around her elders. The nickname that fell to her, Addie, irritated her a little for she liked the name Adaline and hoped one day to lose the nickname. Addie trailed along with Johnny for breakfast.

"You surely can, and I will take my hat off for the little miss to join us also." Boots whipped his hat off as he stood and slightly bowed toward Addie. Her cheeks reddened when she blushed. She enjoyed the attention, but it did not come often.

"Adaline, I believe that is your name. Am I right about that?"

"Yes, but almost everybody calls me Addie," she made a slight frown when she said the word.

Boots took special care of his ability to pick up on the smallest things whether it be with animals or people and he noticed the little expression.

"Well, if you don't mind, I would like to be able to call you Adaline. Of course, if that is alright with you."

The young girl smiled at Boots and barely uttered a yes. She was taken by Boots' behavior immediately. When she sat, her eyes stayed on the mountain man and she watched his mannerisms. She tugged at her father's sleeve and leaned into him to whisper.

"Who is he? I want to know everything about him."

Adaline did not stand apart from others when they looked at Boots. It became a common comment to say they wanted to know everything about him. Boots exuded the idea of what a mountain man is supposed to be. She could not hold her question any longer.

"Why do you like to live in the mountains?"

The question slipped out of Adaline's mouth before Johnny Ross could react.

"Addie, we are joining Mister Mc Cray for breakfast if you don't mind."

"It is fine Johnny. I like having conversations at breakfast, especially with pretty young ladies."

Again Adaline blushed and her eyes fell on the table. She could not look up.

"I sure would like to tell you why I like to live in the mountains if it is alright with your father."

Johnny Ross nodded his approval.

"Adaline, have you ever heard a Steller Jay's call? It is a shook, shook, shook, sound. One lit on my arm and started singing before he realized his mistake. Have you seen how fast a mountain lion can run down a deer? Did you know a coyote cannot outrun a mountain lion? The coyote has many calls. I have heard them all. Have you seen a wolf run? Their tail is straight out the same way a dog's tail is when he runs. Why is that? Have you ever heard an elk bugle? Have you heard geese honking their arrival as they slide across the flat blue waters of a lake? I enjoy all those things when I live in the mountain. I am free up there. Nobody tells me what to do, but there are things I must do so I can live day to day. There is peace up there. It can be so quiet you can hear leaves falling to the ground. That is why I like to live in the mountains." The conversation broke up when Cookie put plates of food in front of them. Boots tucked in to eat his standard fare of steak, eggs, bacon, sausage, biscuits, and cream gravy. A pot of coffee joined the plates and Boots filled his cup. He took a sip of coffee occasionally and he watched Johnny and Adaline as they ate their breakfast.

2

Three men came into the café and they sat at the table next to Johnny and Addie. Two men sat with their backs to Johnny and Addie. One of the men scooted so far back on the bench, the handle of his pistol jabbed Addie in the back. She moved closer to Johnny to avoid the pain of a jab in the back. The man responsible noticed she moved and he turned his head to look at her. While she had her back to him, he noticed her shiny brown hair and the fair skin on her arms. Addie chose a sleeves dress when she dressed for the day. Her chores would be inside cleaning rooms today.

Boots took notice of the disheveled man as he looked at Addie. He finished his breakfast and sipped his coffee. Boots enjoyed mornings like this one. The weather turned out pleasant. Rain for the past few days muddied the street, but the sunshine would soon take care of that. Henry Black sat at the table facing Boots. Stanley Watkins sat with his back to Johnny, and Joe Watkins had his back to Addie. He would turn his head and look at Addie's back frequently. Boots did not care for the three men, he guessed they were outlaws of some sort looking for a place to hide. All three men needed a bath. They smelled of sweat and horses. The gun butt belonging to Joe Watkins poked Addie in the back again and she turned to see what could be causing her the back pain. Joe Watkins turned and looked at her. He grinned at Addie. "Well now, aren't you a pretty little thing? I don't guess I could convince you that I would be good company for you."

Boots stood and looked at Joe Watkins. "That is right. You would never be good company for her. Why don't you scoot on down on the bench? Your pistol is poking her in the back." Boots had seen Addie stiffen when the pistol poked her back. "I am so sorry if I caused you any discomfort little lady."

Watkins moved on the bench giving Addie plenty of space. Boots sat down thinking he needed to keep an eye on those three men. Not much time passed before the conversation between the three started getting louder and louder. The language became fowl and more suitable in a saloon. They were messy eaters, and one of them ate with his fingers.

As they finished, Joe Watkins turned and put his hand on Addie's shoulder and he squeezed hard enough to cause her to wince.

Boots had enough.

"Take your hand off her and you and your little buddies get out of here."

Joe Watkins fought a lot. He didn't win all of the fights, but he figured he could take this fellow who dressed in buckskins.

"Who do you think you are? You can't order us around. Where did you come from with those clothes? Are you a half-breed? I hate half-breeds."

Boots did not like the word half breed used in that manner. He had two children with his Cheyenne wife Migisi and they would be considered half-breeds. No one ever called them that, and he resented being called one when he wasn't.

Boots stepped around the table and grabbed a fistful of Joe Watkins' shirt. He easily lifted the hundred-fifty-pound man and set him on the floor that served as a walkway between the rows of tables. He learned long ago, most of the winners in a fight struck first. So, he drew back his right fist and slammed it into Watkins' jaw. Joe's face contorted something awful and his two friends heard teeth breaking. Joe did not hear a thing because his eyes rolled up in his head and he fell to the floor. The punch knocked him out cold.

"You can't do that to my brother." Stanley Watkins rose to meet the left hand of Boots. He left his boots and flew over the table into the lap of Henry Black. The two Watkins boys were out of the fight.

"If you want some of this, step right up. I have one waiting for you and you can join these two on the floor."

"I am going to stand up, but I don't have a dog in this fight, so don't waste your hand with me."

"Get your two friends up and get them out of here and don't come back. If you ride by this place don't even look over this way. I will come find you."

Henry Black grabbed hold of the collars on both men and began to drag them out of the Flapjack Café.

Henry looked in the direction of the door to the kitchen to see the big Old Cookie standing there with a sawed-off double-barrel shotgun resting in the crook of his arm. He pulled harder thinking this was no place to be at the moment.

Boots put money down for his breakfast, and he included enough to cover Johnny and Addie's as well. Addie stood with her mouth agape at what had just taken place. Boots stepped back to talk with her.

"Adaline, I am sorry you had to see all of that. Those fellows were beginning to get out of hand and they left their manners somewhere else. I don't think they make their momma's very proud."

He looked at Johnny with concern on his face.

"I don't think we have seen the last of them, so keep a close watch on things for a while. At least until we know for sure they have pushed on."

"I will do that very thing. And, I want to thank you for defending my daughter's honor. That happened so fast I did not get a chance."

"No thanks needed. I did everything you would have done if you had seen what I saw."

The three walked out of the Flapjack Café and stood on the boardwalk while Johnny and Boots looked for the three men who had left before them.

Not seeing them, Boots put on his hat and bid Johnny and Adaline goodbye.

The Watson brothers and Henry Black were camped about three miles outside the little village.

"You two look like you stuck your head into a momma bear's cave and she didn't like it."

Henry laughed as he looked a Joe and Stanley.

"Stan, if you had kept your mouth shut, you would have been able to walk out of there without that goose egg on your jaw."

"I am gonna go back and snatch that girl. Did you see her eyeing me? I know she wants to come with me. There ain't no doubt about it either, I am gonna help her get out of that place."

"Joe, if you do that, you are a dead man. That mountain man thinks a lot of that little girl, and if you take her, he will hunt you down and make sure you are dead seven times over. Stan, you need to talk some sense into your brother's head. I think he got his noggin rattled with a fist of that mountain man."

"I am gonna do it. You watch. I am due me a woman. I have not had anybody since I growed up, and I am due."

Joe lay out on his blankets with his feet facing the campfire. He soon fell asleep.

"We are going to part company, Stan. I don't tolerate those who harm children. We have been together for a long time, but this is it. I am packing up in the morning and heading back south."

"Wait just a bit, Henry. I didn't say I wanted to take that girl. That is an idea that Joe has. I don't want to have anything to do with it either. If I can't talk him out of it in the morning, I will ride out with you."

The night's sleep did not change a thing in Joe's mind. Brother Stan talked to him away from Henry.

"Joe, you can't be like this. You need to get that girl out of your head because it means nothing but trouble for you. Henry wants to ride on because he doesn't want to be a part of anything like what you have planned. If you don't change your mind and come with us, I am afraid I will ride with Henry."

"Don't leave me, brother. We are blood and I am the youngest. You are telling me that you will go off and leave me here because I want to do something. Well, if that is the case, I will help saddle your horse because I am staying. You don't know how it is for me. I need to have a woman in my life and that girl they called Addie is going to be the one. I saw the way she looked at me. She wants to leave with me. She is beautiful and I plan to take her."

Before Joe could finish talking, Stan put the bridle on the horse and got ready to saddle up. He turned to his younger brother with the thought he might never see him again.

"I will tell mother about this, Joe. But, I will keep quiet about it if you come along. Now, I am saddling and we will leave you here with the camp."

Stan and Henry walked their horses to a southern path and mounted.

"I am sorry, Stan, but I can't be a part of what Joe has planned."

"I can't either Henry. I don't know what has come over him. I guess this is the last time I will see him."

Joe and Stan were raised together and they worked as a team. This marked the first separation of the brothers. Stan turned in his saddle to have one last look. He saw Joe standing near the fire with his hands at his side watching the two men ride away.

"You just go on then. You don't know me at all. I am going to do this. You will see when I bring that girl home to mother."

Joe snuffed the fire and cleared up the camp. He wanted

to camp a little closer to the little village. Finding a spot where he could watch things would be good he thought. Joe settled on a campsite that showed signs of previous use. The fire ring remained and brush cleared around the campsite. Joe decided he would hang out there.

3

Adaline finished her chores for the morning and snuck out the back door with a plate of scraps. She was supposed to put the scraps in the wooden bin, but raccoons and other animals were in there and she didn't like them at all. Addie found a wooden bowl and put the scraps into the bowl. She did this several days in a row and the scraps were always gone. She thought she might stay awake some nights to watch to see what comes to get the scraps. Tonight would be a good night to watch with the moon full and the clouds were gone. The stars were shining when she sat on the back steps of the hotel. The steps led the way to the privies. One for men and one for women thought Addie. The wooden bowl sat on a rock ledge about a hundred yards from the steps. She wanted to stay awake, but occasionally she would catch her head falling to her chest. Addie jerked herself awake.

When the sky started to get a little lighter, indicating the sun felt ready to show itself, Addie saw movement near the bowl.

A brush line ran alongside the ledge where she placed the bowl. Addie saw a wolf take a tentative step into the clearing around the bowl. Addie could see the eyes of the wolf. The hair coat seemed to have a bluish tint. It could be the light she thought. The wolf looked directly at Addie before he stepped to the bowl to eat the scraps. As he ate, the wolf would raise his head and look at Addie.

Adaline carried the type of personality that could communicate with animals. She spent a lot of time at the corral near the blacksmith shop so she could be around the horses, mules, and burros. When she first discovered the animals were responding to her, she was not talking to them. When she started talking to them, she felt they started to communicate with her through their actions. One day Addie crawled over the fence and sat on the back of a horse that had positioned himself close to the fence. The horse started walking around the corral. Addie pressed her knees to the side of the horse and he picked up his gait. She learned if she wanted him to go left, a little pressure with her left knee would tell the horse to turn left. The same went for the right side. Addie enjoyed that day on the back of that horse. She used no saddle and no bridle. She tried to come to the corral as often as possible, and every time the horse would move to the fence so she could ride.

Her mother Sara wondered where her twelve-year-old independent-thinking daughter might wander off to so often so she followed her one day and watched as Addie climbed the fence and rode around the corral on a beautiful horse. Sara knew Addie did not know about riding horses, but the horse seem to be taking her directions without question. When Addie got ready to dismount, the horse would move to the fence. Addie stood on the back of the horse as she climbed over.

"Well, now I know why you come home smelling like a horse. Adaline what in the world are you thinking? You climbed the fence to get into a corral of rough horses. You could be hurt in there."

"I know, but the horse I am riding would never let that happen. He likes carrots and sugar. Especially the sugar, mother."

Lizzie walked out back tending to the horses with a serving of hay and she saw Addie climbing on the back of the horse and jumping over the fence.

Lizzie's hand flew to her mouth. Lizzie ran the stables and corrals. She took care of the wagon train horses when they came in and saw to it when they needed to have new shoes. Many of the wagon masters told Lizzie the animals came out of her care a lot better off than when they went in. Occasionally, a wild uncontrollable horse would be left behind. The horse gave too much trouble during the wagon train journey. Such was the case with the horse Adaline rode in the corral.

Lizzie caught up with Sara and Adaline as they walked toward the hotel.

"Addie, I saw you on the back of Big Red. Did you know that horse is wild? Nobody ever rode that horse, and when I saw you standing on the back of Big Red I nearly lost it. He could hurt you, honey. I don't know how you managed to stand on his back, but I would never do it again.

I have been around horses all my life and I love them. But, that is one critter I give a wide berth to when he and I are in the same pen."

"It's fine, Lizzie. I have been riding that horse around the corral for a long time now. We get along fine and I don't think he would like it if anything happened to me. We talk to each other."

Lizzie saw right away Adaline possessed a special quality that few people did. She could communicate with horses. Lizzie possessed the same thing, but not on the level as Addie.

"The next time you are down here, come get me before you get on that horse. I want to watch."

"I don't know how he would feel about somebody else watching us."

"That is fine and I will make sure he can't see me."

Lizzie knew few people possessed the ability to communicate with animals and she anxiously awaited the opportunity to see Addie with Big Red. She did not have a long wait. The next day she saw Addie and her mother making their way to the livery.

"I hope to be able to ride today. I don't know if he will feel my nerves because I am nervous that people are going to be watching. He and I were on the sneak before, so no guarantees."

"That is fine, just don't let things get out of control where you might get hurt."

"Oh, that will never happen, Lizzie."

Adaline waited until her mother and Lizzie were well hidden in some trees near the corral. She climbed the fence where Big Red walked to meet her. She managed to get over the fence and nudged the big horse forward. Addie rode the horse in the corral for a long time. She showed how the horse would turn in her direction, and she convinced Big Red into a trot. Addie enjoyed this ride more than all the others because she proved Big Red did not have the personality of a monster horse.

"That ride came out incredible."

Lizzie walked to meet Addie.

"I did not know that Big Red had that kind of behavior in him. We have seen him throw riders over the fence. He has bitten several people. He throws his head a lot, but today he seemed so calm and collected. You are a good influence on Big Red."

"I sure like him. I am not sure I could own him though.

Maybe somebody will come along that will match up with him."

Several days passed and an eastbound wagon train from California stopped at the trading post. A cowboy who wore clothes more suitable for going to the dance put his arms on the fence railing and watched the horses in the corral. Lizzie kept busy tending to her chores.

Addie happened by, not intending to ride Big Red, but she wanted to watch the other horses.

The California cowboy told Lizzie that he would like to take that Big Red horse out for a ride, and if things worked out, he would buy the horse. Lizzie warned the young man about the personality of the horse.

"To my knowledge, nobody has been able to keep a seat on that horse. Maybe you could be the first one."

The cowboy grinned at Lizzie when he told her that was just his kind of horse.

"Let's saddle him up. I like the looks of him. He parts his hair on the right side."

Lizzie pointed out the four white feet.

"You know what they say about that don't you?"

"Never heard anything about it, but the horse looks good with four stockings."

"Well, from what I have heard is this, if there is one white stocking, you better buy him...two white stockings and you better try him, three white stockings leave him alone, four white stockings go on home."

The cowboy laughed at the old saying.

"I never heard that and I don't believe it. Let me saddle that Big Red horse."

The cowboy finally cinched the saddle on Big Red. He had a big whelp on his shoulder from where Big Red tried to take a bite out of the cowboy's hide.

"You will pay for that big boy."

The cowboy pulled on the cinch even harder. Once he was satisfied, he put his left foot in the stirrup and he had to hop to stay up with the horse, but the cowboy managed to swing his right leg over and slip into the stirrup. He produced a quirt to use on the horse.

Addie put her hand to her mouth as she stood next to Lizzie.

"You better get your father down here because it won't be long before that cowboy needs a doctor. I hope he doesn't use that quirt."

Lizzie left the gate open but Big Red shied away, not wanting to leave the corral. On the second circle around, the cowboy put the quirt to use, hitting the horse in the flanks so hard big whelps showed up instantly.

"Lizzie please put a stop to him. It is not right to beat a horse like that."

The cowboy went sailing over Addie and Lizzie's heads about that time. Big Red followed the man to where he landed on the ground and it looked as though he planned to stomp the cowboy.

Addie could not stand what she saw.

"No," she yelled. Big Red heard her voice and turned his head to see Addie standing by the gate. He walked to her as she put out her hand. Big Red was breathing hard. Puffs of breath fell on Addie's outstretched hand.

The cowboy who cut a nice ditch in the dirt where he landed managed to sit up and watch the exchange between the horse and the girl.

"Get that little girl out of here. That horse is a killer and she will get hurt for sure."

The cowboy jumped to his feet and charged Big Red. The horse cow kicked the cowboy. Not much force came with the kick, just enough to keep the cowboy at a distance. Lizzie walked over to help him up.

"Stay away from the horse, fellow. Addie knows what she is doing."

Addie pulled a carrot from her pocket and started feeding Big Red. While he munched on the carrot, she led the horse back into the corral and closed the gate. Once the gate was secured, she put her foot in the stirrup and swung up on the horse. Big Red splayed out all four feet and froze. Addie patted him on the neck and shoulder and talked to him in a quiet voice. He eventually stood up and started walking.

"I have never seen anything like that in my life. I have been riding horses for a long time and I know them pretty well. I liked that Big Red horse, but nobody is going to take that horse away from that girl. I have seen it all now."

The cowboy slapped his hat against his leg to get rid of the dust.

"My father is the doctor here. He can tend to your shoulder for you. His office is next to the hotel."

"Thank you, but I think I might need the pain for a reminder that I don't know everything I think I know. Bless that girl riding that horse."

As Sara and Adaline walked past the Flapjack Café, Joe Watkins stepped out from beside the building.

"Hello, little girlie. I have been watching you." Joe Watkins waved his fingers at Addie.

Adaline stepped behind her mother to move to the other side to be away from the man. Addie and her mother started walking fast toward the hotel. Once inside, Sara let out a breath.

"My goodness, who was that man Addie?"

"He and two other fellows were in the café causing trouble and Boots kicked them out. Father knows all about it." Addie went on her way to get an early start on the next day's chores.

"Johnny, what do you know about three men in the café?"

Johnny explained to Sara about the fracas that broke out and he told her of the warning Boots gave him about watching Adaline.

"One of the men had a fixation about her and he made some threats."

"We saw that man at the corner of the café. He told Addie that he has been watching her. It frightened her, Johnny. I think we better keep a close watch on her."

The hotel was filled with people from the eastbound wagon train. The cowboy that tried to ride Big Red came in for a room.

"I need a good soft bed to put my shoulder on. That hoss took a big chomp on it. I don't think he broke anything, but it sure felt like it at the time."

Sara flipped the register back around to see the cowboy's name.

"Doc Henry will be in here in a minute to look after a sick baby. I will send him by your room."

"I didn't think I needed a doc, but I am rethinking that idea right now."

The cowboy took the key to his room and unloaded his gear. He sat on the edge of the bed and rubbed his shoulder where Big Red took a try and supper. He heard a knock on the door and Doc Henry walked in.

"What is this about a shoulder injury? Pull your shirt off and let me have a look."

Doc Henry saw teeth marks on the front and back of the man's shoulder. He poked and prodded much to the discomfort of the cowboy.

"It looks like that horse intended to throw you over the barn with that bite."

"Oh, he did throw me over the barn. Not with the bite, though, he did not like me sitting on the hurricane deck so there I went."

Doc Henry chuckled as he rubbed a soothing salve on the bite marks.

"I am going to give you a little dose of laudanum to help you sleep, but that is all you get. I will leave some of the salve with you to put on your shoulder."

"That feels a lot better already. How much do I owe you, doc?"

"A dollar will do, but more than that I want you to listen to my daughter the next time she gives advice."

"I will certainly do that...one stocking, by him, two try him, three leave alone, and four go home. That horse had four stockings."

Doc Henry laughed as he left the room.

Addie finished getting her chores ready for the next day and she rested in her room until dark. She rounded up the scraps to take out to the wooden bowl, but she needed a little rest. She napped fitfully as she recalled the cowboy whipping the horse with a quirt.

4

"She is gone." Sara tried to shake Johnny Ross awake.

"She is gone, Johnny. Wake up and go find her."

Still in his sleep, Johnny sat on the edge of the bed trying to get the sleep out of his eyes and head.

"What are you talking about Sara? Who is gone?"

"Adaline is gone. Please go find her and bring her home for breakfast."

Johnny set about getting dressed. As he pulled on his boots, he let out a flurry of questions.

"How do you know Addie is gone? Where could she have gone? Is she at the livery stables with that horse?"

"I don't know, Johnny. I just know she is gone. Addie stays up late some nights sitting on the back steps. I looked out at her before bed and I saw her sitting there last night. I went to wake her for breakfast this morning and she is not in her room. Her bed is made up from yesterday. Johnny, she is gone."

Sara started crying prompting Johnny to hold her and give her assurances that Addie could not have gone far and he would find her and bring her to breakfast. When Sara's sobbing started to calm, Johnny released her and started for the front door of the hotel. Sara remained to get her desk duties done. She could not function well with the fear that Addie was gone. Sara recalled the awful man that stepped out beside the café yesterday when they were heading for the hotel. She thought, what if he got her last night? Sara dismissed that thought, knowing Addie would have raised a ruckus if anybody tried to take her against her will. Sara could not sit behind the registration counter. She went to the lobby and started rearranging things. The California cowboy came down the stairs to ask Sara where he could find a good breakfast. She told him about the Flapjack Café. She noticed he carried his left arm bent to his stomach and he moved with careful purpose.

"How is your shoulder today?"

"It is better today than yesterday. That salve the doc gave me helped a bunch. I know that your daughter rode that Big Red hoss. I feel funny being bested by a little girl, but she knows horses."

"Yes, Adaline has a way with most animals. It doesn't take her long to get a connection with them."

The California cowboy put on his hat and left for the Flapjack Café.

Johnny went straight to the livery where he found August and Lizzie. August hammered on some horseshoes while Lizzie held a horse waiting for the shoes.

"I am trying to find Addie. Have you seen her this morning?"

"No, Addie doesn't come down here until about midday. She told me you were a stickler for her finishing her chores first thing."

"She is right about that and that is why I am here. Addie has gone missing. Her chores have not been done, and Sara says she did not sleep in her bed last night. If you see her, please send her home."

August and Lizzie both said they would tell her. Johnny turned to walk up Flapjack Street when he almost ran into Boots.

"I am looking for Adaline. Have you seen her?"

"No, I came from the trading post and stopped by the Flapjack. I have not seen her today."

Johnny told Boots about the man they had trouble with in the café confronting Addie and Sara the day before.

"He has threatened to take her, and I am afraid that is what has happened."

"I hope she is around somewhere. Keep looking and if we don't find her, I will go after her."

Boots did not want to spend a lot of time looking for Addie in the usual places. He knew if she had been taken he needed to get on the trail soon.

"Take me where Sara last saw Adaline last night."

Sara showed Boots the steps at the back of the hotel.

"She sat on that top step many nights watching the moon and stars, I guess."

Boots took a seat on the top step and looked around. He saw bootprints coming and leaving next to the back of the hotel. He looked out and saw the bowl resting on a ledge.

"What is that bowl out there, do you know?"

"Adaline took leftover scraps out there to feed some animals. I saw her do that one night very late."

Boots told Sara to sit on the top step while he investigated. He saw wolf prints leading out of the brush to the bowl and back into the brush. He knew a wolf came to eat the scraps. Seeing the boot prints told him someone took Adeline. He did not voice that to Sara or Johnny, but rather he told them he would go on the hunt and he would be bringing Adaline home soon. As he scouted the area, he found a camp near the back of the hotel where someone stayed for an extended amount of time. Nothing at the camp gave Boots any identification, but he guessed the man sulking around would be Joe Watkins. There were signs that only one man walked around the fire pit.

Watkins made a row in the café and Boots knocked him out in a fistfight. The man threatened to take Adaline and that caused the fight. Boots wondered if Joe Watkins stayed by himself, or if his brother and the other man were around as well.

5

Adaline watched the wolf step out of the brush line and carefully approach the bowl of scraps. When no interference appeared, the wolf started eating.

Suddenly, Adaline felt a hard rough hand close around her mouth and an arm around her waist. Hot whiskey breath hit her ear.

"I got you girlie. Now don't start throwing a fit. I want that you should come with me."

The man pulled Adaline from the steps and she started to struggle to free herself from the strong hold. She kicked and bit hard.

"You stop that now, you hear? I ain't gonna hurt you none so just ease up and everything will go a lot better. I am Joe, don't you remember me? You gave me a come-on look in the café the other day. I am here now so stop fighting."

Adaline continued to kick and bite. Joe finally realized he would get nowhere with the girl because of her fighting him. He doubled his fist and hit Adaline on the side of her head. The punch put Adaline out for a while. Joe put the unconscious girl over his shoulder and headed for his horse which he hid in the bushes.

Joe managed to get mounted with Addie riding in front of him. She did not regain consciousness.

"I hate that I had to hit you so hard, girlie, but you fight like a wild cat."

He spurred his horse east giving the little village a wide berth. He reached the wide track that ran up the mountainside and he kept his horse moving at a fast pace. Joe Watkins did not know the mountains, the forest, or anything at this elevation. He managed to find a site that showed use as a camp. He stopped, put blankets down, and lay Adaline close to the fire. He watched her and hoped that he did not do much damage when he hit her.

When Joe had his back to her, Adaline would open her eyes just enough to see. She felt a headache coming on, but she knew she would be alright in time. She watched as Joe set up the camp. He pulled some jerky from a saddle bag and sat on a rock near the fire to watch Adaline. She quickly closed her eye so he would not notice she regained consciousness.

"First chance I get, I am on the run," thought Adaline. "I will not let that man touch me again."

As dark set in, Joe tried to get Adaline to take some water. He finally poured some on her face. He heard somewhere that would wake somebody up from being knocked unconscious. Adaline felt as though she were drowning and she sat up.

"Well, there you are girlie. I thought I might have hit you too hard, but here you are now. You sit there and chew on this jerky a bit. Here is a cup of water to go along with it. We need to have a little talk about things, but you need to clear your head first."

Adaline thought to herself that her head cleared long before this man's head cleared. She looked at him with disgust.

"What do you want from me? I am twelve years old and I am not supposed to be here. My father will come looking for you and you better know your day will be bad. I want you to take me home."

"Now lass, I can't take you back. You left with me and you will stay with me. Together we can raise a family and have a good life. That is what men and women do isn't it?"

"I am not old enough for that sort of thing. I barely know how to cook. Take me home and I won't tell a sole where I have been."

Joe laughed at Adaline.

"No, little girlie. We are having ourselves a little get-together tonight."

He pulled a bottle of whiskey from a bag and opened the bottle.

"I am going to pour a little of this in your cup and I want you to take a swaller. It is the top-of-the-line stuff, cost me extra to get the good stuff, but nothing but the best for you."

Joe poured the whiskey into Adaline's cup and turned the bottle up to guzzle a drink. When he did Adaline spit the drink she took. The whiskey burned her mouth and a trickle when down her throat burning a path the entire way to her stomach.

"This stuff is the best ain't it? I know you probably drink from the top shelf, but this is really good for where I come from."

"I don't drink whiskey. I told you I am twelve years old and I am not ready for this kind of thing."

Adaline threw the rest of the whiskey into the fire causing a flare-up. She surprised herself with the jump in flames.

"If it does that to the fire, think what it does to your stomach."

Joe laughed and took another guzzle from the bottle.

Adaline thought "Good for him. He will get stupid drunk and I will be able to walk out of here. I hope we are not too far from home."

Joe settled back on his rock and eyed Adaline.

"You sure are a pretty thing. I can pick a good one, yes, I have a good eye for women. You come over here and sit next to old Joe."

He patted a spot next to him on the flat rock.

"I think I will stay here on the blankets."

"Alright, I will just come over there where you are."

Adaline felt her blood run cold. She did not want to be near this man.

"If you try anything with me, I will scream to the high heavens. You will wind up with a hole in your head too."

"Awe now don't talk that way. Old Joe is your friend. Didn't I hear you called Adaline? I may have to change that name. It is a little too high falutin' for my taste. I will come up with something good for you. How about the Horse Woman? I saw you riding that red horse and you looked really good up there. What do you say to that?"

"My name is Adaline and it will stay my name, and get your hand off my leg."

Adaline felt happy that she wore a man's shirt and pants. She intended to ride Big Red in the getup. She grabbed Joe's gnarly hand and jerked it from her leg.

"Now don't be that way. We are up in the mountains and we are friends. I intend to have my way with you. It can be easy, or it can be rough. I like the easy way best and I think you will too."

Joe reached under her shirt and grabbed her breast.

Adaline let out a blood-curdling scream. She heard sticks and branches breaking and suddenly Joe's hand disappeared. Something knocked Joe to the ground and as he lay on his back, Joe looked up to see the teeth of the meanest wolf he ever saw. Joe did not see many wolves before this day, so this ranked up there with the meanest. The wolf growled and snarled at Joe's face. He took a mouthful of the front of Joe's shirt and started pulling him into the woods.

Adaline heard growling and Joe screaming as the wolf attacked him. Joe finally fell silent. Adaline wondered if the wolf killed Joe. Things happened rather quickly, and Adaline was not sure but she thought the wolf looked like the one that came for the scraps.

The wolf returned to Adaline's side and looked her up and down. She knew for sure the wolf ate the scraps. The wolf panted hard. Adaline poured some water into a big cup and the wolf lapped it up. Once he finished with the water, the wolf turned to face the direction where he dragged Joe, and he put his belly to the ground.

"Well, I see you intend to stay awhile. I thank you for getting that ugly man away, but we are going to need to go home pretty soon. I am sure there are some scraps to put in your bowl."

The wolf turned his head to look at Adaline as if to say we need to stay here for a while.

Adaline admired the big wolf. She wasn't sure about such things, but she thought the wolf would weigh nearly two hundred pounds. Joe would not stand a chance with this wolf. Adaline lay on her blankets and stroked the strong back of the wolf.

Sometime during the night, Adaline woke thinking she heard someone walking. The wolf stood on all fours and she saw the hair on the wolf's neck standing up. He was ready to attack.

Sure enough, Joe appeared at the edge of the trees.

"Little Missy, are you alright? That wolf liked to have taken my arm off."

Joe stopped suddenly when he saw the wolf standing next to Adaline.

"Oh Lord," was all Joe could say as the wolf charged. Joe turned to run for his life. Adaline heard branches breaking as Joe tried to get away from the wolf. He didn't get far before the wolf lunged at Joe's leg and took a big bite. Joe screamed again.

Eventually, the wolf returned to Adaline's side. He lay in the grass facing the direction where he chased Joe.

Joe tried to get to the camp a third time. This time he used his head. He circled so that he would walk up behind the wolf. He wanted to get to his pistol. The wolf could smell Joe a hundred yards away. The whiskey bottle spilled its contents and the aroma wafted through the camp. However, the wolf had Joe's number. He stood and walked around the fire and lay in the grass again. Adaline watch the wolf with the hair that looked to be a light grey, almost blue in the night.

This time, the wolf let Joe get to the camp before he made his presence known.

"Where did your little puppy go? Left you all alone did he? Well, Uncle Joe is here to take care of you."

Those last words came out as Joe spotted the wolf and he yelled at Adaline over his shoulder. Adaline almost laughed at the plight of the man who attacked her. She no longer possessed any fear. The wolf would be her constant companion, at least until she got home.

Boots followed the prints of the wolf and he discovered hoof prints also. He thought the man who took Adaline was being stalked by that big wolf. He noticed the paw prints were as big as his hand and they pressed into the dirt indicating the wolf weighed a lot. Boots thought he had never seen a wolf this size and he looked forward to eyeballing him. He traveled quietly through the forest. The sun wanted to take a peek, but it was early still. Boots heard Adaline scream and he stepped up his walk. Shortly after that, he heard a man let out a scream. It was undeniable that he heard a man. All sorts of things ran through the mind of the mountain man. The wolf attacked the camp and Adaline first. Of course, he would go after the weakest of the two first. But why attack the man? He saw the yellow flame through the trees and he made a slow approach.

Hiding behind a big tree, Boots poked his head around and he was stunned by what he saw.

Adaline sat up on some blankets with an enormous wolf lying next to her. She brushed the hair on his back with her hand. She would occasionally rub the wolf behind his ears, and the wolf seemed to be enjoying the attention. Stuck on trying to decide what to do, Boots eased to within talking distance of the camp. He wanted to get Adaline's attention without alerting the wolf.

"Adaline, it is Boots. I have come to take you home."

Adaline froze for a moment and then turned her head in the direction of the voice.

6

daline saw Boots and she jumped up and ran to him. The guardian wolf did not take a step. He lay comfortably in the grass. Boots looked over Adaline's shoulder to watch the wolf while she cried her eyes out. Once she settled, Boots put his hands on her shoulders and pushed her back so he could look at her.

"Have you been hurt anywhere?"

"No, he grabbed me once and I may have a bruise, but my friend put a stop to him molesting me."

Adaline turned and looked appreciatively toward the wolf.

"Adaline, that is about the biggest wolf I have ever laid an eye on."

"He is pretty, isn't he? I have been putting scraps out for

him behind the hotel. I was watching him eat when that awful man grabbed me from behind."

"Where is he and who is he do you know?"

"He kept telling me his name is Joe. He tried to come to camp two or three times, but the wolf made sure he stayed away. The last time he ran off, I saw blood on the back of his left leg. I know wolf tore into his arm pretty good. Wolf could have killed him. I wonder why he didn't."

"Animals are funny sometimes. Wolves generally don't attack us, people. He just wanted the man to leave you alone. I guess his idea worked out well because the fellow is gone. I heard his horse headed down the mountain. I hope he was riding."

"I want to stay here with wolf tonight. We can go home in the morning if it is alright. It is late anyway so we might as well stay."

"It is fine with me if you want to wait. It will be a long walk for you and you probably need rest. Throw those blankets in the fire. I have some that don't smell as bad as those."

Boots found a pot and went to the nearby creek for water. It was the moment Joe was waiting for. When Boots returned, he saw Joe Watkins standing with an arm around Adaline's neck. Joe produced his gun and pointed it near Adaline's head. Thinking she was safe, the wolf left Adaline's side.

Joe's arm held Adaline so tight she could hardly breathe.

"If you make a move, this gun goes off."

"Now that would not be the smart thing to do, Joe."

The voice coming from Boots sounded calm and friendly.

"Yeah, you don't think I am smart, do you? Well, I got the drop on you now mountain man."

"Let the girl go. She is the one you want anyway. Point the gun at me. I am the one you want to shoot. If you shoot her, you are a dead man. If you shoot me, you might be able to get away."

Joe thought on the words for a moment, and he moved the barrel of the gun in the direction where Boots had been standing. While he thought about it though, Boots moved to a different spot and no longer stood in front of them. Joe moved the gun back to the side of Adaline's head. She whimpered as he tightened his hold on her.

"You quit moving around like that. Missy and me are leaving and you better stay right where you are."

Joe started walking backward bringing Adaline with him. Joe backed into a tree. He hit the tree hard. A hand appeared out of nowhere and grabbed the gun. It left Joe's hand and he felt a sharp blow to his head.

Joe didn't have time to react. His eyes rolled up and he fell to the ground sound asleep. When the grip left Adaline's neck she bolted for the campfire. When she turned she saw Boots turning Joe to his belly. Several pieces of leather were being used to tie Joe's hands behind his back. Boot sat the sleeping Joe up with his back to a tree and he wrapped a rope around him and the tree to make sure he would stay secured.

Boots saw Adaline standing by the fire with a hand to her mouth.

"I did not hear him and he grabbed me from behind again."

"It is alright now, Adaline. I have to say he doesn't give up easily. This time we have him, though. I am going to see if I can find his horse."

"No, don't leave me here with him."

"He is all trust up to where he can't get loose and I won't be gone long. We are going to need that horse to get out of here."

Boots disappeared in the trees and true to his word, he came back leading the horse that belonged to Joe.

"I have decided I don't want to stay here any longer."

"That is fine with me. It will take a little longer to get home because it is dark and we have to be careful where we go."

Boots started clearing the camp and packing things away.

"You and I will have to walk. I am putting him in the saddle."

Boots hoisted Joe into the saddle. He pulled a dirty

kerchief from a saddlebag to use as a gag, and he tied it around Joe's mouth.

"I don't want to hear a word out of him when he wakes up."

Ropes held Joe to the saddle and Boots led the horse to the wide track. He and Adaline walked together. Boots noticed movement in the trees next to the wide track. The big wolf stayed hidden but also stayed beside them as they walked down the mountain.

"Anytime you feel the need, just let me know and we will stop. The clown in the saddle will wake up soon."

Boots heard mumbling from the man on the horse and he turned to see Joe with his eyes open and his face contorted such to reveal he did not have many happy thoughts about his predicament.

"I could rest a little bit. I have been tired ever since we made that camp up there."

The loss of adrenalin made Adaline feel like she needed sleep. She did not want to sleep, but she knew it would be something she needed. Boots found a spot near the track opposite the wolf. Adaline rested on a log while Boots tended to the horse.

"You came up here tonight, fought with that man and now we are walking home, but you don't seem to be tired at all."

"Living in the mountains causes a fellow to push himself to the limit. Since that happens, he winds up with a lot of energy. I have better wind up here. When we get down to the trading post, I start feeling lazy and want to just kind of lay around. Right now, though, I could climb to the top of this mountain without stopping."

Adaline marveled at the strength of the mountain man. Her breath came short of air when she was on the mountain. She wondered if animals like horses and wolves faced the same problem.

"Why does that horse breath normal when we have to breathe in a lot more."

"It may be because their lungs are a lot bigger, but I do know the higher they go, the harder it is for them to breathe until they adapt to the elevation. It seems to me that they adopt a lot quicker than we do."

Adaline stood feeling a little rested and she joined Boots on the wide track to continue their journey down the mountain.

Again, Boots heard mumbling from Joe.

"If you don't stop that stuff, I will stuff a dirty rag in your mouth to shut you up."

Joe leaned forward in the saddle and rested his chest on the pommel. It didn't take long for him to realize that would not be a comfortable position because the movement of the horse caused the pommel to move.

7

"**S**tanley, why are you stopping? We have a long way to go to get to the next little trading post."

"I know where we are, Henry. I just can't go off and leave my little brother like that. I am thinking about turning back and seeing if I can get him to come along with us."

"You tried that and it didn't work. Even if you get him to come along, the next skirt he sees he will lose control of his mind. I don't want to be around somebody that thinks that way. And, I don't want to be around somebody that might hurt a child. If you turn back, I will go on to the next trading post but don't try to catch up with me. I will travel by myself."

"Well, you go on then. My brother is my blood and

since he is younger, I am supposed to look after him. I am going back."

Stanley Watkins turned his horse around and started to backtrack.

"Joe Watkins, I would not want to face your mother right now. She would whip us both over this. I gotta figure a way to turn your head around."

After a day's ride, Stanley reached the Flapjack Café. He sat at a table near the front door. He sipped coffee while he waited for his food. The talk in the café happened to be the capture of little Adaline Ross. When he first heard the words mentioned, he picked up his listening.

"I feel sorry for the man that took that precious little girl away from her family. They haven't left the hotel because they are hoping she will be able to come back some way."

"I know about these things. I read a lot about them in the Sacramento newspaper. They never come back. She will be found years from now and from what I read, she will not want to come back. That happened to that girl in Texas. She lived with the Indians for such a long time, she didn't want to go back to her family. When they found her and took her home, she escaped to be with her Indian family. That is the way these things turn out. I feel sorry for the family, but they best move on. They will have another kid."

"I bet they didn't have Boots Mc Cray on the trail. That

mountain man won't let up until he finds them, and woe be the day for that man. Boots don't tolerate those who cause harm to children."

"I didn't know that about him. I have never seen him raise a hand to another man."

"You should have been here when he took on three of them, and one of the fellows gave Adaline the look. I bet he is the one who snatched her. He talked dirty around her."

Stanley took the last sip of coffee and left the Flapjack. Old Cookie was left standing with a plate full of food in one hand and a pot of coffee in the other.

"That man just left out the door. Who wants this food?"

"Did he pay before he left? If he did, I will take the plate."

"No, there is a charge on the plate."

"One of the men from the wagon train held his hand up to signal Cookie he would take the food."

"That's Old Cookie for you. A banner day today, he gets to charge twice for a plate of food." The men at the table laughed, and Cookie gave the jokester a pat on the back. That pat turned into a hard slap on the back.

"You are paying double today, too, Buster. Just get your pocketbook warmed up because most of it will be in Old Cookie's pocket before this day is out." The table erupted in laughter as Cookie turned to walk back to the kitchen.

"He did it. I can't believe my little brother. He did it. I have to find him and get that girl back to her family and get him out of here. Something tells me we are both in trouble. I gotta see to it the boy has a chance to turn his mind around."

Stanley worked his way to the back of the ceilings. He did not want to be seen because he felt as though some people might recognize him and cause trouble. He worked his way toward the trading post. From the east side of the building, he saw a man and a girl walking toward the trading post. They were leading a horse with a man in the saddle.

"That has to be Joe. He is trussed up like no other."

Stanley snuck to the west wall of the trading post so he could watch what happens next. He recognized the mountain man named Boots leading the horse. The girl walking beside him seemed to be fine to Stanley.

"I guess we will find out what Joe did. That is the girl he wanted to take."

Boots told Adaline they would walk to the hotel first. When they reached the front, Sara screamed.

"My baby is here. Adaline has come home."

Sara froze with joy standing in the lobby of the Kit Carson Hotel. Johnny had taken a walk to the river, still looking for his twelve-year-old daughter. People in the lobby heard about the disappearance of Adaline and they moved to Sara's side as Adaline climbed the steps.

"Mother, I heard you scream. I am home. Yes, I am home."

Sara took Adaline in her arms.

"It was a happy scream, Adaline."

Both started crying. The people in the lobby were patting Sara on the back and telling her congratulations. Sara did not hear a word because she became focused on Adaline.

"Where have you been child, and why did you leave me?"

Boots stood on the steps with the hotel door open.

"Adaline was taken by the man on the horse. She tells me she is fine, but I would suggest you have Doc Henry check her over. She spent some time on the mountain and there are fleas and ticks up there. Those little bugs can cause all kinds of sickness."

"Thank you, Boots. Are you the one who found her?"

Boots did not get a chance to answer before Adaline started talking.

"Yes he did find me, Mother, and he took care of me the whole time he was there. Thanks to him, I was able to get away from that man."

The entire little village heard about the rescue of Adaline. Among them, is Doc Henry. He took Sara and Adaline to the infirmary to check her over. There, Sara learned about the wolf. Every time Joe Watkins tried to do something to Adaline, the wolf ran at Joe and inflicted damage. Doc Henry conducted a thorough exam and cleared her of any problems to be concerned about.

"Whew, Adaline. Doc Henry pronounced you a tough girl. I am proud of how you handled yourself."

"I wished the wolf would have come too, but I don't think he likes a lot of people being around. I want to take some scraps out tonight and see if he shows up like usual."

"That is a great idea, but maybe somebody should be with you. I don't want to go through this again."

Johnny learned of his daughter's rescue when he stopped to talk with Boots at the livery. Boots discussed plans for Joe Watkins.

"He took my daughter. I have a plan for him. Turn him loose and let him run. I will have some target practice. The man does not understand things the way he should. He will probably wind up taking somebody else just as he did with Adaline. He needs to be put out of his misery."

Several men from the eastbound wagon train were nodding their heads agreeing with Johnny Ross.

"String him up." One man said loudly. A chant started as a result.

"String him up, String him up." The chanting continued until Boots raised both hands to get their attention and quiet the crowd.

"We are not going to string him up. We are going to see what the law has to say about Joe Watkins."

Stanley stood in the back of the crowd. He could not hold it in any longer.

"There ain't no law against what he did. He took a

woman to be his wife. It is done every day. Half the men in this part of the country would be in jail if there was a law against it."

The crowd started murmuring. "Maybe he is right. What law did he break anyway?"

"I think the sheriff needs to come out here and either take him in or cut him loose." one man allowed. Boots nodded to the man.

"You may be on to something there fellow. I have him under my watch. You folks need to settle a bit and let the law handle Joe Watkins.

"Is that his name?" A tall man dressed in all black stood in the middle of the group of men.

"If that is Joe Watkins, there is a paper out on him and his brother Stanley for robbing a bank in Tucson."

"Lock him up, lock him up." Another chant started in the crowd.

"I think that is best. I will lock him up until the sheriff gets here."

Stanley decided he needed to be elsewhere and he sneaked away.

"We are both in trouble now. Maybe I can break him out and we can put some ground between us and this place."

An empty storeroom behind the trading post became a temporary holding cell for Joe Watkins. There are no windows and it was dark, but a cot and a chamber pot were the only two items in the room so Joe could pace the floor.

After securing Watkins in the store room, Boots convinced August to ride to town for Sheriff Riley. The sheriff knew of the people at the trading post and he favored most of them. He knew the wagon trains usually contained a miscreant or two so he paid particular attention when a call for law got sent out. August wasted no haste getting to town.

"Sheriff Riley, we are holding a man who took a child from her mother and father. He went to the mountains with her. Boots tracked them down and brought the girl home and the man is locked in a storage room."

"Did the girl get hurt in any way?"

"She says no because his attempts were interrupted every time he tried something. Doc Henry said she had some bruises, but that is about all. Her parents are Johnny and Sara Ross. They run the Kit Carson Hotel."

"Yes, I know those folks. The little girl's name is Addie. Do I have that right?"

"Her full name is Adaline. Somebody shouted that papers were out on Joe Watkins and his brother Stanley for robbing a bank. We don't know about that, but I hoped you would."

The sheriff opened a drawer in his desk and pulled out a stack of wanted posters. He shuffled through them.

"I need to clean this drawer out, but you know a lot of

the times we don't know if somebody has been caught, so I keep them all. Let me keep looking."

Eventually, the sheriff found a poster for Stanley Watkins for robbing a bank in Tucson. He set that one aside and kept digging.

"Here it is. Joe Watkins for bank robbery with his brother Stanley. There is a five hundred dollar reward for each one of them. Let me get my deputies lined out and we will ride out there together. I am sure Addie would like to be five hundred dollars richer."

Sheriff Riley smiled.

"Has anybody seen Stanley? He is usually close by according to this paper here on him. It reads that he looks after his little brother. So maybe we can get him as well."

"Joe is no little brother. He is a good-sized man, but he may be a little short upstairs."

Sheriff Riley rounded up two deputies. One is supposed to accompany him and the other he told to watch the store while he goes to capture a vicious criminal. He turned to August as they strode out the door of the sheriff's office.

"August, I don't think I can do anything to him for taking little Addie that way, but he is going to jail for a long time. I will see if I can think of some extra law that he broke to add a little time for him."

"I had that suspicion there were not any laws that he broke taking her. She is twelve years old and I have heard of girls that age getting married. People in the wagon train wanted to hang him or shoot him for what he did, but we thought the law should step in."

"I am glad calmer heads prevailed. My poster doesn't say dead or alive, just alive. So it is good that he is still breathing."

8

Stanley returned to the campsite where he, Henry Black, and Joe slept before breaking up. He got water for coffee, started a small fire, and put the water on to boil. He ate some jerky that he soaked in the hot water. The water tamed the toughness of the jerky. Stanley thought he had enough jerky to make a pair of boots because it was so tough. He settled in to drink his coffee when he heard the clop of a horse hoof on a rock. Stanley set his cup down on the fire pit ring and he quietly went to hide behind a tree.

"Stanley, are you here? I saw your old horse a ways back and I circled till I saw your camp. Come on out so we can talk."

Henry Black dismounted and pulled the saddle from

his horse. He rubbed the horse down with clumps of grass, then led him to a place where he could graze. After hobbling the horse, Henry returned to the camp.

"Why are you here, Henry? You swore you would never see the Watkins boys again. So, what gives?"

"I got to thinking about it, Stanley. We have been riding together for a long time. A feller ain't much of a feller if he rides off when one of his partners needs a little help. I come back to see if there is anything I can do to help you out of your jam."

Stanley told Henry the story.

"He took that little girl we saw in the café. That darn mountain man they call Boots tracked him down and brought Joe and the girl back. They are holding Joe for the sheriff. He is in a little building behind the trading post and I was just thinking about going up there and busting him out."

"We can go in there after dark and maybe take the door off that building. Nobody with see us."

"I don't know about that Henry. These people are pretty smart about things like that. There may be a guard there or something."

"We can go in and take a look."

Henry and Stanley sat around the campfire and talked about plans for where they would travel next.

"There is a little town west of here. I would like for the

three of us to go take a look. I bet there is a bank there holding our money. We could make a little cash withdrawal."

Both men laughed.

"There is nothing better than old friends around a campfire drinking coffee and talking about things. But, I sure miss my little brother. I cannot imagine him thinking he could get away with taking somebody's kid like that. When I saw him tied to that horse, blood had run down his leg. It looked like he was some kind of tore up. That mountain man did it to him. I wouldn't mind plantin' him before we go on."

"Stanley, we have not killed anybody that we know of. I shot one inside that bank in Tucson, but I just nicked him. We don't need to be going off and killing people. It just ain't right to do that. Robbing banks is not so bad. We spend the money right back. I think of it as kind of giving the town a little boost in business. Those banks don't need all that money so that is something we are doing that is good."

"Sometimes I think the three of us should get a reward for what we are doing. Wouldn't that be nice to get enough money so we can go home and buy a piece of land to make a living? I am getting a little tired of all this roaming around that we are doing. If we do that, maybe my brother can find himself a wife."

Darkness fell and the moon found Stanley and Henry

at the little building where Stanley knew his brother Joe had been placed. A padlock secured the hasp that held the door closed.

"These people are not very smart. You see the hinges are on the outside of the door. All we have to do is knock the pins out of those hinges and we can open the door. Find us something to use."

Henry stood looking at the door. He could hear noises coming from inside the building.

"Are you sure Joe is in there? I can hear something. Put your ear up to the door."

Stanley bent his head so he could listen.

"That is Joe. He is sound asleep and snoring. I recognize that snore."

Henry found a piece of wood and a rock to use to see if the pin in the hinges would come out. He started knocking on the wood with the rock. The pin did not move.

"This thing is so rusted, I don't think a piece of wood is going to help. We need some metal of some sort."

"I know, there is a blacksmith shop down the way a bit. I bet we can find something around there."

Stanley and Henry went looking for a piece of metal to free Joe Watkins from the confines of the little building. Stanley and Henry laughed at the stupidity of whoever built the building because they put the hinges on the outside. It would only be a matter of time before they freed

Joe. While they laughed, Stanley and Joe were talking in their normal voices as though no one could hear them. They were wrong.

Boots took his turn watching over the storage building. He wanted the first shift so he could have a little sleep. Boots lost a night's rest when he rescued Adaline from the clutches of Joe Watkins. He heard the conversation between the two men bent on freeing Joe from the building. Boots realized Stanley and Henry would try the hinges, and he hoped they would. He carried the key to the padlock on the door, and he would be happy to use it to unlock the door and throw the two men inside. Johnny Ross came to Boots' hiding spot. He took the second watch shift.

"Glad you are here. I am waiting on the return of Joe's brother and another man who thinks we are stupid because we put the hinges on the door on the outside. They are looking for something to knock out the pins. They went to the blacksmith shop to see if they could find something that would work. When they come back, let's you and I take them down and put them in there with Joe. Sheriff Riley will be happy when he gets here in the morning."

"How do you know all this, Boots?"

"Well, they are the stupid ones. They talked loud enough to raise the dead. I could hear every word. We will wait until they return."

. . .

STANLEY FOUND the perfect piece of metal to knock out the hinge pins. He planned to use a rock as a hammer.

"When we get him out of there, let's ride for the flatlands and get as far away from these mountains as we can. I never cared for the mountains anyway."

Henry Black spent a good portion of his adult life in the mountains during trapping season. He told Stanley there were good things about the mountains, such as the abundance of game animals for food, and there were some bad things about the mountains, such as the winter blizzards. He agreed to move on south once they freed Joe from the building.

Three taps on the piece of metal knocked the pin of the upper hinge loose. As Stanley bent over to work on the lower hinge, he saw moccasin feet. He took a brief moment to think "Oh no, we have been caught" before a whack on the head brought stars and little birds cheeping. Stanley fell to the ground, out like an empty lantern.

Henry held the door in place as the hinge pins were to be knocked out. He heard Stanley go to the ground and he looked over his left shoulder to see what happened. At that particular time, Henry felt a whack on the head. His hat fell to the ground about the same time Henry made it. His face fell into his hat.

"Johnny, I believe we have captured two stupid men.

Here is the key if you will do the honors of unlocking the padlock, I will put that top pin back in so we can open the door and throw these two in the building."

When the padlock snapped open, Boots had the pin back in and he carefully opened the door a couple of inches. He looked in and saw Joe Watkins still sawing logs. Johnny Ross smiled at the scene.

"How can a man sleep through all this racket out here?"

"I don't know, but his fellow inmates can ask him."

Boots handily put Henry Black on the floor of the storage room by lifting him by the collar and the top of his pants. He reached for Stanley Watkins to grab his arm and drag him inside. Once both men were inside and joining Joe Watkins, Boots pulled out his pistol and fired a round inside the storage room. All three men scrambled to hide in a corner. The blast of the gun in close quarters had a deafening effect on them.

"You boys better listen here." Boots stood with one foot on the door trim, the other on the ground. "I am only going to say this once. You three have pulled some stupid stunts in your day and with this last one to break out Joe takes the cake. Sheriff Riley will be here in the morning to take you all to jail."

Boots turned to Johnny Ross.

"We got them, Johnny. I think we can go to bed and get a little rest without worrying about an escape. Go take care of Adeline."

"I don't have to worry about her. Sara is sleeping in the same room with her for a while. She can't go to sleep very easily without her mother in the room with her."

9

August and Sheriff Riley rode together to pick up Joe Watkins. When they arrived at the trading post, Mary told them Boots had the key to the padlock on the storage building. Mary did not know there were two other men in there with Joe.

"He and Johnny Ross are at the Flapjack Café for breakfast. That place has become a second home for my son."

August told Sheriff Riley he could see why Boots spent so much time in the café.

"He knows everybody and they come to see him there. Plus, he doesn't have to eat his cooking. His wife Migisi is staying with the Cheyenne and Boots claims to be a good cook, but he misses Migisi's cooking."

After their greeting, Sheriff Riley announced he missed

breakfast this morning because August showed up with his wagon ready to go.

"I want whatever you are having."

Boots smiled at the sheriff.

"I am having steak and eggs with sausage and bacon. When I finish that, I am having flapjacks with some of Old Cookie's maple syrup. There is a pot of coffee on the table there while you wait."

When Cookie asked the sheriff for his order for breakfast he pulled back a bit.

"I am riding today, so I need to keep it light. How about a stack of flapjacks with that maple syrup and throw in a couple of pieces of sausage while you are at it? I get tired of so much bacon. I like it, but not for every single meal."

"Sheriff, Johnny and I have a surprise for you today."

"I hope it is a good one."

"It is a good one. We have three men locked up in the storage room. Joe Watkins, his brother Stanley, and a fellow by the name of Henry Black are snoring together in there. I am planning on taking one at a time out to the bushes so they can do their business. Mother wants to feed Joe, but I told her that is something you can take care of. She doesn't know Stanley and Howard are in there with him. Johnny Ross and I caught those two trying to break Joe out last night. We threw them in there with Joe and told them to settle down."

Johnny nodded his head at the story.

"I have never heard anything as loud as a forty-five pistol fired in a small building. I was outside and my ears are still ringing. Boots fired a warning shot over their heads. I am pretty sure they are still in the shed."

"How is Adaline? I hope this stuff doesn't bother her too much."

"She is a tough girl, Sheriff Riley. Sara sleeps in her room with her for comfort, but Adaline says that is not necessary. We think it will help her get back to normal. She is twelve years old and she is a fighter."

"Good, Mother and Father can bring her through it. If I hear right, it sounds like your family is handling the situation well. There is a five hundred dollar reward for Joe and the same for Stanley. I haven't checked for papers on Henry Black, but I wager there is a sheet on him as well. I intend to get the five hundred in reward money sent to Adaline. Maybe that might help a little."

"I would appreciate it, Sheriff. We will put it back for her so she will have it if and when she needs it. Sara wants her to attend school back east. Adaline is horrified by the idea. She wants to stay here. We have some time to sort that out."

As they approached the storage building where the three men were locked inside, Sheriff Riley stopped suddenly.

"My nose is telling me there is a stink in there."

"We had one chamber pot in there. I hope they didn't run it over, but these fellows didn't smell as though they had a lilac bath within recent memory."

Boots unlocked the padlock and Johnny opened the door. All three men took a step back because of the odor coming out of the building.

"Let us out of here. Joe has some problems and he is going to kill us all. We can't breathe. At least we are afraid to draw a breath in this kind of air, it will give us black lung."

Henry did the talking. He stood with his hands on the wall on each side of the door. His head was hanging out in the fresh air.

Sheriff Riley grabbed Black's arm and pulled him out of the storage room. He put the man in his irons quickly.

"Boots can you get me some rope and leather straps? I brought only one set of irons thinking I had one prisoner to take back."

The sheriff walked Henry to a cleared area and made him sit.

"Johnny, watch this fellow while I get the rest of them out of that stinking place."

Boots appeared with rope and leather straps.

"Stanley Watkins, get out here. You are under arrest for bank robbery."

"I am coming out, sheriff, but you got the wrong man. I have never robbed a bank in my life."

"Tell your story to the judge. It is my job to make sure you get the chance to clear your name, so come out here."

"Well, since you put it that way, I will come out."

As soon as Stanley reached the doorway, Sheriff Riley grabbed him by the arm and took him face down to the ground.

"This ain't no way to treat an innocent man. I said I would come along."

"I know you will come along now."

After getting Stanley tied up, he helped him stand.

"I want you over there facing that wall, Watkins. If you move, you give me a good reason to shoot you. I want your nose touching that wall."

Boots helped Stanley to the wall and he followed the sheriff's orders by placing his nose on the wall.

"Joe Watkins, it is your turn you are under arrest for several charges, among them bank robbery and stealing a twelve-year-old girl from her family. Get out here now."

"I am coming out, sheriff, but I didn't rob no bank either."

"Well, you just confessed to stealing a twelve-year-old, so get out here now."

Joe did turn out to be the source of the bad smell. He seemed to have forgotten the chamber pot and went in his pants.

Sheriff Riley used the leather straps to tie him up.

"I have to get him to the river so he can wash. I am not taking him to my jail like this. Can you fetch me a pair of pants?"

"I will see what mother has available in the trading post. We can put these two in the tack room at the livery while you take him to the river. The fish are going to be plenty displeased, Sheriff. Even those downstream are going to get a whiff of this."

They walked the men to the livery where Lizzie put Stanley and Henry in the tack room and locked the door. Boots showed up with a pair of pants for Joe Watkins.

"August, we are going to need your wagon to haul these three to jail. I can't chance to put them on horseback. The county will give you their horses and saddles if you will come along with the wagon."

"I don't need more horses, Sheriff, but seeing as how you don't have a way to get them to town, I will take them. The wagon and I will be ready when you get back from the river."

Sheriff Riley and a somewhat meek Joe Watkins walked to the livery stable. The sheriff made Joe climb in the back of the waiting wagon "He don't smell like lilac, but he is not near as odiferous as he was. I left those pants on the river bank. They need to be thrown in the nearest fire. I didn't want to touch them."

Henry Black and Stanley Watkins were pulled from the

livery's tack room and hustled to the wagon. They were still trussed up and both put their chins on their chests so they could stare at the ground. Henry Black complained he still did not get any breakfast.

"I will get you one of those cow patties over there if you don't keep quiet. You will get to eat in due time, but right now, we are going to jail."

August drove the wagon with the three prisoners in the back. Sheriff Riley stayed behind the wagon, but he kept to one side to stay out of the dust. It seemed as though August found every rut and rock for the wagon to roll over. It made for a rough ride to town.

"Sheriff, I have a supply list of stuff to get while I am here, so if you need me for anything, I will be over to the general store."

"Thank you for your help, August. As soon as I get these three in cells everything will be fine. I will set up the arraignment for tomorrow, but there is no need for anybody to come in for that. I plan to set that telegraph up with the trading post so we can communicate. It will make things a lot easier for me and those folks around the trading post."

He took one prisoner at a time into the jail and put each one in a different cell. Sheriff Riley sent a deputy to fetch breakfast for the new prisoners.

On the ride back to the trading post, August thought

about how the telegraph did not get the use that it should. We could have sent for the sheriff with a telegraph message instead of me riding to town to fetch him. We did that so much, it never crossed our minds to send a telegraph message. Maybe next time, August thought.

10

August found Boots filling packs to put on the pack burro. The only time Boots wanted to use a pack burro was those times when he went high up the mountain trail. August stood and watched his brother make his preparations to leave.

"I am headed up early in the morning. I plan to spend some time with Migisi and her people, then I want to go on up to my cave where I left all my belongings."

It was Boots' way of saying he wanted to go home. He lived on the high lonesome and utilized a huge cave as a cabin. The cave could handle a family easily. A small underground stream came to the surface for about fifty feet in the cave before returning underground. Boots claimed that water possessed healing powers, and he also claimed the water had the sweetest taste of any water. His hunting gear, buffalo robes, and cooking utensils were hanging on hooks made into the wall of the cave. A large depression in the rock porch served as a convenient place for a bath. He heated water in a big cauldron next to the depression and took hot baths in the middle of winter. Boots made his home in that cave, and when he left, he always wanted to return.

The journey to the Cheyenne village where Migisi stayed with her mother and father, Chief Ehane took two days to reach. Migisi stayed with her mother because her age began to take a toll on her health. Migisi knew she would take care of her mother during her last breath. She taught Migisi all the healing powers possessed by the matriarch of the chief's family. Her brother Red Feather stayed close by as well. Chief Ehane looked twenty years younger than his real age and seemed to have no heal problems. He credited his wife's healing powers.

Once underway, Boots looked forward to the journey. He left Migisi behind and he did not return for many months. He felt anxious to see her again. Boots and Migisi met at a young age when Boots trapped beaver. They wound up at the Rendezvous at the same time and eventually eloped. That is when Boots learned the daughter of an Indian chief does not elope. He suffered at the hands of Red Feather when Chief Ehane came to take his daughter home. After a time, the chief appeared again at the camp where Boots stayed. This time, Red Feather did not come along. The chief told Boots that his daughter and her mother were very unhappy. They wanted Boots to marry and live in the Cheyenne village. Boots agreed to the marrying part, but he told the chief he would not be able to live in the village. The chief expressed his disappointment but agreed if Boots would come with him. Boots did not know the exact location of the Cheyenne village. He had an idea, but those kinds of ideas could get a fellow killed in the mountains. Chief Ehane and daughter Migisi helped ensure the open arms welcome for Boots. He learned to enjoy their cultures and their lives. Things seem to fit with those of a mountain man.

Finding the traditional waypoint campsite, Boots removed the packs from the two burros and led them to a small meadow so they could graze. He did not care for the feel of a saddle, but he put that aside for the necessity of convenience. His kit was easily tied to the latigo on the saddle. He pulled things off the saddle to set up camp and then unsaddled the horse. He unhooked the lead on the rope halter and the little mustang followed him to the area where the burros were grazing. After hobbling the horse, Boots returned to the campsite and surveyed everything around it.

"With all this stuff, the packs, the saddle, the kit, it looks like I am setting up home here instead of staying the night."

He unrolled the canvas and spread it on the ground

where he put his blankets. Boots scouted for wood to build a fire. He remembered the teachings of the Cheyenne fire building. If you build a big fire, you freeze. Build a small fire and stay warm. The theory being the big fire consumes all the wood at hand. A small fire would mean less scouting for wood. Boots thought someone before him built a big fire. It took him some time to find enough wood for his camp.

Another lesson he learned was to get pots of water before getting the fire started. Otherwise, burning wood while getting water would be a waste. The camp sat about a hundred yards from a small stream. Having camp close to a noisy stream could prove to be dangerous. The noise of the water might cover the approach of a friend or foe. As he reached the stream, Boots could hear the water tumbling over rocks. The stream was not very deep, but the water rushed and the bottom of the stream showed clear. He kneeled on the stream bank and filled water in two pots. Boots made his way back to the camp noticing the quiet of the woods. His vision and awareness were getting back to the normal state for Boots. When he stayed near the trading post, the noise of all the activities of mankind dampened the sharpness of eye and hearing skills developed in the mountains. Boots sensed a return of the familiar abilities.

The small fire crackled and warmed the two pots of

water. A dump of coffee in one of the pots soon sent out an aroma that Boots favored.

"There is nothing like campfire coffee." Old Cookie at the Flapjack Café kept a pot on a campfire behind the café building just for Boots' morning coffee.

Flat stones and logs were brought up at some time or other to provide seating around the campfire. Boots sat against one of the logs and sipped his coffee. He noticed some forest noise returned. Usually, when men worked their way through the forest, the birds, squirrels, and other creatures became aware and would either leave or get quiet to stay hidden. Mountain man Boots Mc Cray became so aware of the creature's habits, he learned to sneak through with his moccasins on his feet for stealth, so he could fool them. He listened this evening for the noises. Boots recalled the conversation that took place with Adaline when she asked him why he liked the mountain so.

"Adaline, have you ever heard a Steller Jay's call? It is a shook, shook, shook, sound. One lit on my arm and started singing before he realized his mistake. Have you seen how fast a mountain lion can run down a deer? Did you know a coyote cannot outrun a mountain lion? The coyote has many calls. I have heard them all. Have you seen a wolf run? Their tail is straight out the same way a dog's tail is when he runs. Why is that? Have you ever heard an elk bugle? Have you heard geese honking their arrival as they slide across the flat blue waters of a lake? I enjoy all those things when I live in the mountain. I am free up there. Nobody tells me what to do, but there are things I must do so I can live day to day. There is peace up there. It can be so quiet you can hear leaves falling to the ground. That is why I like to live in the mountains."

11

Boots heard the ceremonial drums miles away from the Cheyenne village. He smiled to himself remembering Chief Ehane searched for ways to have festivals to keep the enthusiasm in the village as high as possible.

"It can get very boring here and bad things happen when people are bored," the chief told Boots. "Festivals provide enjoyment, but one must be careful, too many festivals can also become boring."

Chief Ehane proved his wisdom in many ways. Finding reasons for festivals seem to be a strong point.

Boots stopped momentarily to listen to the drum beat. He knew Migisi stayed behind to care for her mother who drew close to death. He wanted to make sure the drum beat he heard was not a ceremonial drum beat for death. After hearing more, Boots felt assured the drums were signaling a festival.

As he drew within sight of the village, Boots could see people lining each side of the main thoroughfare. It was as though they were expecting a parade. He stopped his forward progress not wanting to interrupt goings on. Red Feather came to his side and gave him the Cheyenne greeting.

"What is the festival about, Red Feather?"

"My father is expecting your arrival. We have been waiting many days for your return. We have had successful hunts and there will be a feast when the moon rises."

Red Feather clapped Boots on the back and put out his left hand, indicating the folks were waiting for Boots. Once Boots started walking he did not realize Red Feather took charge of the mustang and burros.

Boots remembered the lines like this in the days marked with war. A tribal custom for captives would be to line the thoroughfare and the captive must run the gauntlet ending at the ceremonial fire. Most times, the captives never made it that far. He knew this would be different because the people were welcoming him home.

As he entered, both sides rushed to him to pat him on the back. After a few yards of people continuing to pat him on the back, Boots began to feel as though those pats were becoming rather heavy at times. He wondered if he would make it to the end of the line. He could see Chief Ehane dressed in his glorious regalia. The colorful headdress nearly touched the ground. Two young maidens held the end of the headdress to make sure the last feathers would never touch. That would signify the death of the chief. The two maidens were honored to be chosen to hold the feathers because it meant they could prolong the life of the chief.

Next to Chief Ehane stood the chief's sick wife. Her face was drawn and she appeared as though she had aged years. Migisi had her arm around her mother as if to hold her so that she would not fall.

Boots wanted to be with his wife, but a few things must happen before he could talk with Migisi. Chief Ehane greeted Boots and launched into a long speech about the legendary mountain man returning home. And, several times, the chief mentioned the need for a great feast. Once he finished talking, Boots made his way along the greeting line to reach Migisi.

"I have missed you greatly, wife. How have you fared in my absence?"

"I have fared quite well in your absence, my husband," Migisi joked.

Their back and forth became an integral element of their relationship.

"Even so, I am overjoyed you came to see me. You should follow me to our lodge so that we can speak freely. I must see my mother to her bed. She wanted to see your arrival."

The drumbeat stopped and people started going about their daily business. Boots agreed to visit with the chief before the feast. When Migisi returned, she took him by the arm and led him to the family lodge.

"Tell me first of our children. I have longed for them."

Boots told her Little Boots and his sister Ayasha continued the operation of the Whispering Pines Ranch. Little Boots secured a contract with the government to supply horses, and the children and the ranch are well. Boots recalled the purchase of the Whispering Pines he counted as an accomplishment. He liked the countryside, and the ranch lay south of the trading post. Plus, with Little Boots and Ayasha running the outfit, he could return to the mountain.

Boots and Migisi enjoyed bringing each other up to date about events. Red Feather put his head in the lodge to tell Boots the chief wanted to talk. When Boots emerged from the lodge, he realized a lot of time passed while he and Migisi talked. Darkness fell and the celebration festival started.

Boots and Chief Ehane sat side by side during the ceremony. The pipe was passed around and all the elders took part. They all nodded at Boots after passing the pipe to the next in line. Once the pipe was finished, the chief launched another long talk about the legendary mountain man

Boots Mc Cray. The elders heard the stories before, and they noticed how the chief added some excitement to the tales and smiled knowingly at Boots. Boots would put his head down at the polishing of the truth, but the Ehane was the chief, and if he wanted to embellish a story, that came to be his privilege with the position.

"I marvel at how this man could kill only half of a deer. After a hunt, he came with only the back half of a big deer. I saw him and thought the deer must have been too big to carry and he left the other half. I later learned he split the deer with another hunter because they both fired at the same time and neither knew who killed the deer. I thought a name for him would be One Who Killed Half a Deer, and then it came to me the real matter. This man gave half of his bounty to another man so the other man would have food for his family. It is the kind of man that he is. We have never known the name of the other hunter."

One of the villagers raised his hand to the chief. The old hunter came through some very hard times losing members of his family by sickness and accident. Boots knew of the man's hard times and wanted to give him the whole deer, but the man would take only half. Boots thought the chief might be honoring the wrong man.

"You see that man lives today through the gift of this mountain man."

The festival went on for hours, and Boots retired before

the events finished, but he already earned a pardon from the chief.

Boots stayed in the village for three enjoyable days. On the third night, Boots found his packs full and set by the door.

"I guess this means you are kicking me out again."

"I am because you are ready to go. I have been with you a long time and I can tell when my man Boots is ready to move on. You must understand I will be staying here with my mother. Her days are numbered, but we do not know the number. When the time comes I will travel to our home at the cave. Red Feather will have your horse and burros ready for you to leave early in the morning. You must leave before sunrise, otherwise, it will be difficult for you because your friends will want to spend more time with you. I know you are ready to go, and I am ready for you to go. I want you to find that peace you are wanting."

Boots knew he chose the right person to be by his side for the rest of his life. She raised their two children, she put up with his escapades, and she fought by his side. Migisi is the right person for mountain man Boots.

Boots traveled the game trails well. He found a park where he could stop at midday. He took the four-legged animals to a brook for fresh water. The brook fed into a lake and Boots decided he would take the afternoon to catch fish. He didn't question whether the fish were biting, the storied mountain man knew they would be hungry.

He made camp a hundred yards from the brook and he hobbled the horses in the park so they could graze. They were showing signs of being tired so this would be a good rest for them. He found a long thin branch he could use as a pole. Boots carried a supply of hooks and he tied a long string to the pole and the hook.

"Now for some bait. I wonder what would whet the appetite of a big fish."

Boots watched bears fishing and they knew when to grab. They did not use bait, but he did not possess the skill of the bear so he needed a little help. He dug grub worms from the bark of a fallen tree. Ants were plentiful so he crushed some of them. As he approached the edge of the lake, a grasshopper flew in front of him. Boots managed to catch it.

"I didn't know grasshoppers lived this high up. This fellow happened by just in time to help me catch a fish."

The grasshopper worked. It took some patience on the part of the fisherman, but Boots pulled in a nice-sized fish. Next, he tried the grubworm and immediately caught a fish. The ants did not play out very well, but Boots had enough fish for several meals.

After cleaning the fish near the brook, Boots went to camp. He found firewood close by and soon heard the crackling of the burning wood. First things first for Boots, however. A pot of water went next to the fire to boil for coffee. The fish slipped onto sharpened sticks and they were held over the fire for roasting. Boots chopped some greens and added berries to a bowl. He carried walnuts with him and he chopped some for the greens and berries. When he finished, Boots looked over his evening meal thinking it was a meal fit for a king.

He listened to the night sounds as he lay asleep. Boots had a knack for being half awake and half asleep at night. It is the only way to describe how he rests. He hears things while he sleeps and if anything doesn't sound right, Boots goes on the alert. This night, even those turned out to be more noisy than usual, nothing was out of the ordinary. The stars were still out when Boots woke. He poked the coals in the fire and heated another pot of water for his morning coffee. As he sipped his coffee, he again thought back to the description he gave Adaline about why he like the mountain life. He was ready to experience those things again.

Boots lingered at his campsite. He could take his time to reach his home. He felt sure it was not going anywhere, and he wanted to enjoy the mountain. He decided he would hunt so he cleaned his rifle and packed cartridges in his pockets. The lake provided a good hunting spot. The game would have to come to the water sooner or later, and he was early enough to see them come in this morning. He made his way to the lake and stopped at the tree line. Boots found a tree where he could climb and rest on a big limb with a good view of the bank around the lake. It is in late summer but he would not hear an elk bugle for several more weeks. Boots watched several elk come to water on the far side of the lake out of gun range. Waterfowl did not interest him as he wanted to take a good quantity of meat back to camp. Boots noted on his way to the lake, the spot where he cleaned the fish had been visited by several animals, possums, and raccoons both left tracks. The raccoons were fastidious eaters and washed up after their meal. He could see where at least one raccoon visited the water in the brook.

The sun started to rise, and Boots had a hard time keeping his eyes open since he woke so early. He nearly dozed until he heard stomping in the woods behind him. The noise came closer and closer. Eventually, the rack of a big buck deer appeared under the perch where Boots waited. The shot would be difficult with the deer directly under him, but Boots did not want an old deer such as the one making the racket. He hoped a smaller, younger buck would follow, if not he would settle for a doe. A young buck showed up at the end of the line of a herd of deer. When Boots took his shot, birds made a loud racket with their wings taking flight. The echo of the blast from the gun sounded across the lake waters. Suddenly, one could hear no noise in the woods.

Boots cleaned the little buck and carried the carcass to

camp. He cut off some meat for stew and made backstrap steaks for later. Boots lofted the rest of the carcass using a rope thrown over a high branch. He climbed enough to secure it to a low branch with ropes. Stew makings were boiling quickly and Boots enjoyed his usual cup of coffee. He enjoyed the rest of the day exploring the park and the lake. Boots knew the place well, and he looked for any changes that took place while he spent time off the mountain. Rocky remnants of an avalanche showed up across the lake on a high cliff. The spattering of trees could hardly stop the slide once it got underway. Rubble landed at the edge of the lake and stacked high enough that there would be no crossing at that point. Going around the other side of the lake revealed a waterfall of about twenty feet into a large pool below. Boots thought he might move his camp to the lower pool because he found it remarkably pretty there with all the foliage. Late blooming flowers scattered across the opposite bank.

He made his way back to camp and sat trying to decide if he wanted to spend another day in the park or head to his home. He finally decided he wanted to go home. The night turned chilly. Boots rolled out his blankets about thirty yards from the camp. He knew the smell of fresh meat and cooked meat would provide an open invitation to predators. He did not want to wake up with a mountain lion staring him in the face. Things were calm and in order when he woke the next morning.

12

Boots made good time to the cave that he called home. He built a corral just below the cave that was bordered on three sides by rocky cliffs that stood hundreds of feet tall. The two burros and the mustang found plenty of grass, and a depression in the rocks held enough water. A lean-to on the cave side of the corral would provide cover in times of rain and snow. When the gate closed, the animals were safely tucked away. The saddle and packs were removed and put on the rock outcrop that served as a front porch for the cave. Boots walked around the front on the lower ground and started up a narrow path that led to the entrance.

Bear tracks showed prominently going to and coming from the cave. The tracks were those of a huge bear. Boots thought it must be a big grizzly and hopefully, the tracks leading away would mean the bear is gone. Being an expert tracker, however, Boots thought the bear sought the comfort of the cave for his winter nap. While the air turned colder at this elevation, it seemed to be too early for hibernation. Perhaps the grizzly scoped the place for future use.

Boots eased his way up the path and stood on the porch of the cave so his eyes could adjust to the darkness. He noticed that all of his belongings were located right where he left them the last time he was there. He took a few steps inside. There were two fire pits in the cave. One is located near the mouth of the cave and one is further inside for use during the cold months. He could hear the little stream running in the back of the cave, but his gut is telling him danger lurked further back. Sure enough, as he went deeper into the cave, he saw a giant grizzly curled up sound asleep. Boots quietly retreated to the front of the cave. He wanted to make sure he had an escape route should the grizzly suddenly wake up and charge.

A bear the size of this grizzly would take every bullet a man could shoot and he would still be coming. A gun would provide no help at all.

"He thinks this place is his, and I think it is mine. So, who is going to win out here."

Boots gathered a lot of wood for the front fire pit. He made a pile of rocks sized for chunking. He planned to wake the bear with the rocks and somehow convince the bear he needed to leave and not come back.

The first rock thrown into the cave hit the bear in the rump with little effect. The second rock ricocheted off the ceiling and fell harmlessly on the bear. The third rock provided the expected result. The bear growled and the growl seemed atrocious as it bounced off the walls of the cave. The animal turned and faced the direction from which the rock was thrown. Another rock hit the bear in the head. Boots thought the world may have ended at that point. The old grizzly bounded out toward him as Boots climbed to the top of the ledge overhang. The bear reached the front of the cave with the intent to take care of where those rocks were coming from. Boots threw a couple more from his perch above. The bear turned and saw Boots standing tall with his arms spread out from his shoulders. He made a scream much like that of a mountain lion. The sight of a big object making a loud noise made the bear think twice about where to lay his head for the winter months. He turned and started down the path that led up to the cave. Boots watched the bear until he thought it would be safe to come down. When he reached the porch, the bear sensed something behind him and turned to look.

Boots hurriedly lit the fire in the front fire pit and it roared big very quickly. The old grizzly wanted no part of the fire and the human disappeared into the cave where he could no longer be seen. Old grizzly turned and lumbered down the path on his way to find another place to sleep. He gorged his belly before coming to sleep and he did not have any desire to eat anything else. The horse and the burros were fidgeting in the corral, but the bear paid no attention. Boots accumulated knowledge of the bear's customs over the years. The big grizzly may return sometime next year, and the large fellow found a place to sort of sleep it off after a big foraging meal. He knew bears do not sleep all winter as a lot of the trappers thought. Boots likened their sleep habits to prolonged rest periods. He also knew there would be no other bears in the cave. Grizzlies were especially territorial and had another bear been in the cave or entered after the grizzly went in there would have been a fight to end all bear fights. No evidence such a fight occurred in the cave.

Cleaning up and getting the cave set up as a home site took all of two days and Boots felt ready to hunt for food to store. He enjoyed taking his morning coffee on the rock porch of the cave so he could gaze and wonder at the landscape before him. Off to his right lay a green valley. He watched deer, antelope, elk, and moose travel through that valley. He enjoyed hearing the sounds of the forest. Sing songbirds were few, but some ventured to the high elevations. Squirrels and chipmunks scurried about. If he looked across to the other side, the stilting rocky faces soared. Mountain sheep could be seen climbing to higher places. Boots wondered what made those sheep want to climb in that manner. The food sources were limited until they reached a plateau they eagerly sought.

Boots managed to get up before dawn and he could occasionally glimpse a movement in that valley that gave him the idea a mountain lion lived there. He became concerned about the safety of his horse and burros. One night, Boots thought, he might scout the valley for the big cat. He knew the lion would eventually find the whereabouts of the four-legged animals and he did not want to lose them.

Boots packed a kit and loaded his pack on one of the burros. He did not worry about the other two. They had plenty of grass and water. He closed the gate and led the burro to a patch of ground headed east from the cave. An enormous park provided plenty of nutrients and water for all of those who made their home on the mountain. Boots planned to make camp and watch as the stream of water flowing through the park drew animals in for a drink. The park became his favorite hunting spot and for years, Boots provided for his family with bounty from the park.

An old campsite showed itself to Boots and the site looked like the mountain man might have been the last to camp there. He unloaded the burro and turned him loose. He would not wander far because the grass would be plentiful and woods enclosed three sides of the grazing area. Laying out his kit, Boots decided to wait for a fire. He did not want to eat until later in the day. After collecting enough wood for a later fire, he searched for his spyglass. Boots walked along a trail he made years ago, and it seemed as though others liked the trail because it showed plenty of tracks. The well-worn path led to the edge of the tree line and onto the river that flowed through the middle of the large park. Boots stopped at the tree line and found a place to sit. He saw smoke coming from three fires well away from his camp and they were separated along the outer edges of the park. He looked at the nearest one with his spyglass. The thought he could make out the three men sitting around a fire pit eating breakfast. Deer and elk carcasses were hanging in trees away from the camp. The three men were very successful in their hunt.

The other two camps were so far away Boots could not make out much. He did not see anyone at either camp, but the camps were at the outer range of his glass. He watched the one camp where the three men ate breakfast. He identified two of the men. One man he knew as Trapper John. He and John spent years together trapping beaver on the mountain. The other man Boots knew as Trapper Bailer. The fellow got the name because he seemed to bail on any hard work. The third man kept his back to Boots and he could not get any idea about his name.

He spent the day watching the men he knew as friends. Boots debated the idea of going to their camp and having a reunion of sorts. But, he came to the spot to find peace and tranquility, not to strike up talk with a bunch of old trappers.

That night Boots slept in a cold camp. He did not light a

fire because he did not want to be discovered. If there were to be any discovering, he would be the one doing the discovery. Early in the morning, he decided to make the trek to see his friends. He did not make coffee.

Boots worked his way down to a gully that ran south of the camp where the three men slept. The lazy sun had not made its presence known.

The moccasins helped his stealth and Boots began to feel as though his mountain man skills were returning and maybe getting better.

13

"Boots, if you don't get into this camp and make us some coffee, I think I just might shoot you thinking you were somebody else."

Hearing the voice startled Boots. Not only did somebody know he came close, but they knew his name. Boots stood and put all stealth aside and walked to the camp. Three men lay in their blankets. Trapper John opened one eye and looked at Boots.

"You will find the coffee in that pack by my saddle. As soon as you get the water boiling let me know and I will try my best to throw off these blankets and we can have a talk."

Boots rustled around and found the coffee. Trapper John did not mention where the water pot might be hidden, so Boots searched some more. He found the pot and went to the river for water. As he bent down to fill the pot with water, he felt a tug on the pot, and then he heard the report of a gunshot. Boots fell to the ground and lifted the pot to see a bullet hole in the top by the bail. There would be plenty of water for coffee if he could make it back to the camp.

Crawling on his belly, Boots set the water pot far in front and crawled to it. He repeated this method until he made it to about twenty yards from the camp. He finally grabbed the pot, stood, and ran the rest of the way for cover. He did not hear any more shots fired.

Trapper John sat up on his blankets as he pulled on moccasin boots.

"They have been doing that every dad blamed morning when we go for water to make coffee. That is the only shot of the day, and I am bound to find out who is behind it."

"You could have warned the fellow you sent for water."

"What for? Have you been shot lately? I didn't think so, and I didn't think you would be shot today. Let's make some coffee."

Boots got the coals going and put a couple of pieces of wood on the fire. Soon the water started boiling and Trapper John made four cups of coffee.

"You bunch of no goods need to end your beauty rest. That ain't working for you anymore, so get up and get some coffee. We have company in the camp."

Trapper Bailer sat up and wiped the sleep from his eyes.

"Did Boots finally make it in? I was wondering about what his hold up was coming to see old friends."

The other man kept to his blankets.

"Who is that over there?"

"I guess you never met Whistler. We picked him up a few years back. He is a dead-eye shot with a long gun. He might be as good as you, but I doubt it. Whistler is a bit of a funny fellow. He lightens things up when he is not asleep."

Trapper John picked up a small rock and pitched it at the sleeping man. The rock hit the man's rear end.

"Not again. Every single day I wake up with somebody throwing rocks. One of these days, I am going to start throwing them back."

Whistler grabbed the edge of his blanket and pulled it up over his head.

Trapper Bailer, Trapper John, and Boots drank their first cups of coffee of the day and started the bantering which was normal for these three.

"I know you are going to ask it, so I will just blurt it out for you. We saw the glint off your eyeglass yesterday when you were eyeballing around the river. You are the only mountain man I know that has one of those. You had a cold camp with no smoke. You could have sent a letter over here without your name and we would have known who sent it. We have been expecting you all day yesterday and last night. You finally think you are sneaking in here this morning. I got news for you. Elephants at the circus make less noise than you tramping through the woods. Of course, I have heard all the stories about mountain man Boots. I know you are a legend and I respect that, but hanging down there with those people might have cost you a step or two. I am just sayin', Boots."

All of them laughed at Trapper John's remarks, especially Boots.

"I know I lost a bit. That is what I am doing up here, trying to find where I put it."

More laughter woke Whistler up enough that he decided he needed coffee.

"We need Bailer to get us more water," Whistler remarked.

"If you think I am dragging that holey pot down to the river to get water for your coffee, well, buster, you got another think coming. I am not moving."

"You come by your name quite naturally, don't you Bailer?"

Whistler picked up the pot, went to the river, and returned with more water.

"Why is there only one shot? I thought I was a target there for a bit."

"Whoever does the shooting has a Henry or a Sharps rifle. It is a long way from where we get water to where that shot comes from. In the morning, we all need to be up. I will take the first run and get shot at so you Yahoos can eyeball where the bullet comes from. Maybe old Boots could pull out that looking glass of his and find it. There are two camps across the park. It has to be coming from one of them. Since nobody has been hit yet, I am thinking somebody is having fun with us."

Boots stood and walked over to where the carcasses were hanging from a rope spread between two trees. He counted six of them.

"You boys have had a good hunt it looks like. Two of these for each one of you."

"We had to wait an extra day for Bailer to get his second. He got it the day before you showed up. We were ready to pull out until that eyeglass of yours gave you away. We decided to wait for you to show up, of course, knowing you would."

Trapper John did most of the talking for the three companions. Bailer stayed quiet, and Whistler enjoyed his coffee. Bailer finally stood.

"Trapper John here has us tied in with the Blackfoot tribe on the other side of the mountain. We are going to take this meat to them if we don't eat it all first. I spent my time making the travois for each man to pull. Those two will have to whack everything down to size so we can tug along."

"That is the only thing he hasn't Bailed out on."

Trapper John laughed.

"Before we start whacking though, I want to find out where those bullets are coming from."

The four men left after Trapper John threw his coffee dregs from his cup onto the fire.

Bailer stopped as they started to walk from the camp.

"Should we split up and two go around one side and two go around the other?"

Boots turned to Bailer.

"If we are facing a shooter, that would be a good way to get us all shot and maybe killed, shooting at us one at a time. We need to stay together until we find something and then we can spread out. We stay in the tree line until we reach the first camp."

The sun stood straight up by the time they neared the first camp.

Using his eyeglass, Boots spotted a man cooking with a small fire.

"I will be dammed," Boots uttered.

"Why, what do you see Boots?"

"I believe that is King Charles over there. Here, take a look and see."

Whistler looked confused.

"Who is King Charles? I don't know any kings up here."

14

"He is one of the old trappers. His real name is Charles King. That got turned around years ago and he is now known as King Charles."

"I sure believe you are right, Boots. I want to move in a little closer to make sure, but if it is King Charles, I am hungry. That man can make a French chef give up. He is one heck of a cook."

As they drew closer to the camp, Boots led the way. He heard a voice calling to the men.

"Get in here right now. I have been shooting at you people for long enough trying to get an invite or to get you to come over here. By golly, it looks like you finally got some smart and came over."

King Charles stood so he could be seen by the visitors. He did not stand very tall, and he looked as though he did not eat his own cooking. His clothes seemed to hang on around his body.

When the four men reached his camp, it was glad-handing all around.

King Charles, Boots, Trapper John, and Trapper Bailer knew each other from their days of trying to get rich with beaver hides. Whistler fell right in. While he did not trap with the four, he was a trapper during that time and he worked for one of the fur-buying companies.

It was as though Chief Ehane followed Boots to the camp. Old stories were told and retold, and on the second telling the stories even grew to a legendary quality similar to the chief's talk at the festival.

The five men spent several days reminiscing about earlier times. They ate well. King Charles could also fish and brought in several nice-sized fish from the river. They dined like kings.

"King Charles, we have to whack up some meat to take to some Indian friends of ours. Come with us to our camp and go with us to the village."

"Man, I would give anything to be on the trail with you four, but I must stay here. I am a sick old man. I am not sure what is wrong, but I am sure of one thing, and that is that my day is coming. I want it to happen right here where we are. That camp over there is full of a bunch of hooligans, so watch out for them. They don't bother me at all. I might even go a little higher when winter sets in if I am still stirring around. The bunch of you coming over and us talking about the good days makes a good finish on it for me. I want to go with you, but I must stay, and that is what I will do."

Boots and the three other men left the following day with sadness in their minds and chest. They were sad about King Charles.

Boots spent time helping carve up the meat for the three to take to the Indians. He returned to his camp with enough meat to last him for a while. He did not have to hunt. He packed his burro and started for his home.

On his way, Boots began to see signs that other people were on the mountain. Fresh campsites, tracks made in wet ground, and broken limbs and tramped grass where people walk. He felt the cave would be fine because the signs he saw were well down the mountain from his cave.

"I find it hard to imagine the mountain is becoming populated."

He spent several days close to the cave and he finally decided to hunt in the park below. It would not be a far walk, but the terrain would be rocky and unstable in places. He planned to spend the day.

In the early evening hours, Boots felled a nice elk and he took the elk to the wall that stretched up to the cave. He tied a rope around the hind legs and fed the rope as high as he could. An iron treble hook held the rope on the side of the wall. He fetched another rope from the cave and managed to snare one of the treble hooks. It took him the better part of an hour of hoisting and resting to get the elk to the cave porch. He took the elk to the trees and strung it up for processing. After he finished the job, the remaining carcass went deep into the trees so others may take advantage of the remaining slivers of meat.

Strips of elk meat were on spits to smoke, and he cooked a steak on a makeshift grill he found several years ago. The aroma of the cooking meat filled the cave and Boots became very hungry. While he checked the strips to see if they were done, he heard a voice calling to him. He turned to face the direction of the voice.

"I said hello the cave. Are you hard of hearing? We are starving down here and would appreciate a little food to eat. Can we come up?"

Boots did not like the tone in the man's voice. Something told him the man could be trouble. He did not want him or his people close to the cave.

"Show yourself and I will take some food to you. Do not come to the cave."

"Why can't we come up there? You have a good fire and it could be a place where we could stay for a night or two. You stay where you are and we will come up."

"I said no, and I mean no. I will shoot if you come close. You can take your own meat if you want. I am no longer offering, so you can just leave."

"That don't sound so friendly, mister."

"You are right. I am not friendly and you better leave."

Boots heard nothing more from the man.

Later that evening as he washed his tin plate, Boots heard whistling.

"Now what?" he thought. "He is coming back again."

The whistling stopped for a while and started again this time a little closer. Boots recognized the tune of the whistler. It was a tune the old trappers sang at rendezvous. He knew Whistler, Trapper John, and Trapper Bailer were nearby in the woods.

A shot rang out and Boots heard some of the foulest language a grown man could hear. Somebody was wounded by that shot.

The whistling started up again with the same tune. Boots went into the cave and took two rifles, two six guns, and all the ammunition in a box to the stone porch. He sat on the ammo box with a long gun lying across his knees. A sawed-off shotgun with the barrel sawed short lay on the rock porch next to him. Boots considered himself ready for any eventuality. One thing he knew for certain was that there would be no strangers visiting him this night. He looked up to the roof of the cave and saw Bailer's head.

"There are four of them trying to get up here. Whistler got one and Trapper John and I are trailing them. Sit tight. There may be a circus sometime soon."

Bailer's head disappeared and he could hear the man crawling away from the mouth of the cave.

Boots looked at the strips of elk jerky, forgotten when things started to get tense. He walked to the fire pit and took the strips on the spits and put them on the rocks around the fire pit. There they could stay warm.

Boots could hear crickets to one side of him, but no noise came from the front. That must be where they are, he thought. He knew if they moved to the east, they would find themselves in a rock crevasse and might fall. They were bound on one side by the crevasse, and on the other by the cliff that opened up the park.

"If you are coming, bring it on you fools." Boots took no quarter from anyone, especially someone wanting to threaten his home."

The voice started up again.

"Alright, smart-aleck. Here is the deal. There is one of you and there are four of us. You don't stand a chance against our firepower. All you have to do is say, 'Fine come on up' and we will let bygones be bygones. You shooting one of my men didn't help much, but he is not hurt badly. We just want to eat a little grub, sleep a little bit, and we will be on our way. How does that sound?"

15

Boots knew if the four made their way to the cave they would not be leaving anytime soon, and he would no longer have a life.

"That doesn't sound good to me. Leave and then we will let bygones be bygones. Get on out of here if you value your life. I don't and I won't hesitate to take it either."

A shot rang out and the bullet ricocheted off the top of the cave.

"If that is the best you can do, you don't stand a chance."

Boots finally found a target with a clear shot. He fired and felt the recoil of the big gun against his shoulder. His target took a bullet in the chest and fell over dead before he hit the ground."

The dance had started. Boots heard Trapper John,

Trapper Bailer, and Whistler firing into the brush down below.

"The rest of you boys need to start making your peace with the man upstairs. We have you surrounded. There is no escape."

"You are going to have to fight me first."

The intruder fired a round that hit Boots in the left shoulder. He fell to the ground and worked his way into the cave. Looking at his shoulder wound, he found the bullet went all the way through. While the shot sent pain all through him, Boots suffered worse at other times. He put a cloth on the front side to stop some of the bleeding. He could not reach the backside.

Trapper John appeared at the front of the cave.

"I saw you take a round. Where are you hit?"

"It's a through and through John. It hurts like the dickens, but there are worse things."

Trapper John put the cloth on the backside of the wound and wrapped a bandage around it to keep the cloth in place.

"I think that will hold you, Boots. Trapper Bailer and Whistler are taking care of the rest of those owl hoots. We were coming to see you and they followed us. I am sorry we brought all this to your door, Boots, but we can get it taken care of. I will put some water on for coffee and you just rest."

Boots told Trapper John where the barrel of water sat,

and he leaned against the wall of the cave to rest. Soon, the smell of coffee reached him and he tried to get up to find a cup.

"Sit down, Boots. I felt bad that morning when I sent you for the water and King Charles took that shot. Of course, we didn't know that King Charles fired those shots, but all the same, I still felt bad. Now, here you are with a bullet hole in you coming from some idiots that followed us. Say, is that a strip of elk on those rocks?"

"Get a piece and give it a try. I am not sure it got ready before the big dance commenced, but it may be good."

Fierce shooting broke out on both sides. Boots calculated there were only two of the intruders left, but Trapper Bailer and Whistler seem to have everything under control. He leaned back against the wall again and fell asleep.

After a few minutes of constant gunshots sounding on the mountain, silence came. Trapper Bailer showed up at the entrance to the cave, and Whistler followed.

'I am going to get back the meat they stole from us."

"Good idea, Bailer. While you are out there, see to the burial of those four would you?"

Whistler sat by the fire pit and consumed a piece of elk jerky.

"This is really good stuff. You didn't tell me old Boots could cook."

Trapper John continued to eat his piece of jerky.

"He can't cook. Everything he learned comes from his

wife Migisi. Now that woman knows how to put the pot to the fire. I have never had any better food. I think if Bailer is gone too long, he might need some help. That could be a job to bury four of them. I will stay back and tend to Boots."

Trapper John started worrying about two things. Worrying just happened to be one of John's problems and it was a problem that made him come to the mountains in the first place. Still, the worrying stayed with him.

The first worry is about Boots. He slept a long time, and he doesn't appear to be wakening anytime soon. The second worry is about how long Bailer and Whistler were taking to recover the stolen meat and put those fellows six feet under. He knew that six feet figure might be a tall order on the mountain. Under the topsoil, the mountain turned to hard rock. A fellow would have to find soft ground for a grave.

Trapper John soaked a bandana in cool water and placed it on Boots' forehead. When he laid the cloth across the forehead, he could feel the heat.

"I hope he doesn't catch the fever from that bullet. That would be just my luck to have men following me to this cave and killing the best mountain man that ever lived."

Whistler found Bailer dragging the stolen travois.

"Have you dug a grave for those four yet?"

"Yep, I sure have. They are in that crevasse over there. I put a bunch of rocks on them to keep the varmints away. I hope they don't find them, because those four would make any varmint sick enough to die."

Whistler and Bailer wrestled the travois to the cave entrance. Whistler stepped inside and ask after Boots.

"I am afraid he has gone to the fever rather quickly. It usually takes a few days for it to hit, but I think it is on him now."

Whistler took an interest in Boots as he bent over to look at the wound and test his forehead for heat.

"You boys need to help me lay him on those robes over there and let old Doc Whistler take care of the mountain man."

Trapper John looked at Trapper Bailer. Neither man had any idea Whistler knew anything about doctoring.

16

"You said Doc Whistler, is that right?"

"Right as rain my friend. I spent years doctoring till I got tired of it and found you two. That fever can set in any time it wants, and it looks like he may have a dose of it. We won't know how bad it is for a few hours yet. If you could talk Bailer into bringing in my pack, I have some things in there that may help."

His supplies were limited but Whistler made up a poultice for both sides of the gunshot wound. He cleaned the wounds thoroughly before applying the poultice. Clean cloth covered the wounds and Whistler expertly wrapped the bandages so the cloth would stay in place.

Trapper John and Trapper Bailer looked on in amazement at the skill of Whistler.

"I wondered about you when I saw you cleaning the

two deer you took down. I noticed you looked a long time at the guts and then used that sharp little knife to butcher. I never seen one of those little knives before."

"That little knife is called a scalpel and it is used when a doctor has to cut into somebody. So you can imagine how sharp that thing is. I studied the guts trying to learn what and where those deer were eating."

Bailer looked to be a little confused.

"What did those guts tell you after you studied them so much."

He looked over to Trapper John who was taking all this in.

"Don't ever tell anybody else we ran with a fellow who says that the guts of a deer might talk to him."

"Well, Bailer, studying those guts did tell me something. I know they were eating rich grass and I was surprised to see some parts of nut in there. I guess he picked those up along the ground somewhere. They were from lower down the mountain. The blades of grass were fatter than the thin grass we see up here."

"I will just be durned. You learned all that studying those guts. I don't think I will take that up, but it is kind of interesting to know some of that stuff."

"We need to give Boots time to fight back the fever. He will run hot and cold, so we need cool water and more robes at hand."

Boots lingered in and out of the fever effects, mostly

moaning. He woke enough to tell Whistler his shoulder hurt like the dickens. Doc Whistler gave him a small dose of laudanum and Boots went to sleep quickly. The doc surmised Boots never took laudanum before this very day.

Early one morning, Doc Whistler woke Trapper John.

"I think the fever is breaking. He may start getting really cold, so be ready with the robes. I hope that doesn't happen. If the fever breaks, he could be out of the woods soon."

Whistler hit the nail on the head with Boots. He came out of the coma he was trapped in because of the fever. When he woke, Boots didn't say much other than wanting a cup of coffee.

Trapper John poured a cup and held it to his lips so Boots could sip.

"That is what a man needs coming back from the trip I just took. How many days was I under? It seems like every-thing happened just yesterday."

"Boots, you have been out of it for about a week. You had to have your ups and your downs, but the thing is, you pulled through. We now must make sure that wound gets healed up."

"We found out Whistler used to be a sawbones doctor. He has been looking after you the whole time."

Trapper John stood and smiled at Boots then at Whistler.

A few days later, Boots moved around as though he

never felt the wound. Whistler cautioned him about opening up the wound again because that would cause more problems with blood loss. Boots understood that, but he felt the need to get his strength back.

Trapper John, Trapper Bailer, and Whistler stayed with Boots for weeks. He never tired of their company and they never tired of his. Bailer took much of the meat they processed over to the Blackfeet as soon as the shooting stopped.

"We were late, and they complained a lot, but they still took it. That is a big village and they have a lot of people hungry."

While Bailer stayed in the village, two large hunting parties left to scour the western side of the mountain. One of the parties returned with a heavy load. Bailer did not wait around for the second party to return. The three trappers were friendly with the Blackfoot tribe for many years. Trapper John saved the son of the chief after a snow slide. The young brave wound up buried up to his chest. His leg underneath him was broken. John dug him out and took him home to the village. The three men became friends with the chief after that.

17

Boots woke when he heard the sound of horses and men below the cave. He saw Trapper John sitting up on his blankets. Trapper Bailer and Whistler were still asleep. Trapper John started whispering.

"I think we have visitors. If my ears are true to me there are three horses and three men walking. They must be leading the horses. Now they have stopped below. I will take a look."

Boots held Trapper John by the arm.

"I think I may know who has come. I have been kind of expecting this. The lead man will be a Cheyenne named Harkahoma. He is Chief Ehane's older brother."

"I know the chief, but I did not know he had an older brother."

"Harkahoma stays quiet. He speaks only Cheyenne so

there isn't much outside conversation for him. If you know the chief, you probably met his wife Nokomis."

"I did meet her. She is a beautiful woman with healing powers."

"She is also Migisi's mother and she has been very sick. Migisi stayed with her for many months, but when I saw her last, Migisi told me the end is near. I wager Harkahoma has come for me to go to the Cheyenne village."

Boots stood and walked to the porch of the cave. Harkahoma would not come inside the cave so Boots would always meet him in a grassy area below. When he stepped out on the porch, he recognized Harkahoma and two young braves appointed to travel and protect the old man.

Trapper John heard a conversation taking place in the Cheyenne language. He knew some words but did not stay around the tribe long enough to learn to speak.

After a lengthy conversation, Boots turned and walked inside the cave.

"He is not happy. Harkahoma does things in his way. He came to fetch me to the village because Nokomis is failing. I am aware she is sick and I told him I would go there in due time. He is waiting below for me to go with him. I have preparations to make, and sometimes the Cheyenne don't understand that. They jump on their pony and leave. I have things to pack, I want to find out if you fellows want to go along, and other things like that. I don't jump when Harkahoma wants me to jump. He is very old and his patience is short. I have a lot of respect for him and I thank him for coming all this way, but I will go on my own. So we have an impasse. Harkahoma is camped down below. When I travel with him, there is no stopping. My horse is exhausted by the two-day ride through the woods. He has several horses at hand and can afford to tire his mounts. It is a different life for him and for me."

Trapper John stood nodding his head signaling his understanding of the plight of Boots. He searched his mind for a possible solution.

"What do you think about this, my friend? You get packed tonight and go down there and wake him and you head to the village. Trapper Bailer, Whistler, and I will load your two burros and walk them down. So then we would be there a day or so later."

Boots agreed with the idea and left his packs for Trapper John and the bunch to take care of. He went straightaway to see Harkahoma who fell asleep as soon as he finished talking with Boots. Two scouts sat near the older brother of the tribal chief.

He reached down to shake Harkahoma to wake him when one of the braves grabbed his arm and indicated Harkahoma did not want to be wakened.

"We must leave now. He came for me and I am ready to go."

Harkahoma heard the conversation and sat up.

"You want to leave now?"

"Yes. The sooner we can leave for the village, the better it will be. We have much dark left."

Soon the party got underway.

"How many do you have with you?"

Harkahoma showed signs of sleep overcoming him so Boots thought a conversation would help.

"These two are close by, there are two in front, two behind, and two to each side"

"You brought ten braves with you?"

Harkahoma held up both hands signifying ten braves came on the journey.

"Why did you feel the need to bring so many?"

"Scouts tell me the Lakota are on the mountain and they are angry. Someone killed one of their hunting party and they are trying to find them. I thought they may think we were the one. They found him with an arrow in his heart. It was a Cheyenne arrow.

Boots sat up in his saddle. That news did not sound good.

He heard noises in the woods and thought the accompanying braves may be responsible, but he knew their walk would be quiet.

It had been years ago, but Boots could recall helping Chief Ehane and Lakota Sioux Chief Enapay came to terms with peaceful coexistence between the two tribes. Both of the chiefs brought their people to the mountain to be able to enjoy peace. Tribal warfare became a common occurrence at one time, and they successfully escaped the killing and annihilation of their people. The Cheyenne and Lakota were natural enemies. The Cheyenne were a people who avoided conflict, whereas the Lakota were aggressive. Boots could understand the Lakota wanting to avenge the death of one of their own, but he felt sure the Cheyenne were not the guilty party.

"Did the arrow come from someone you know?"

Boots wanted to be somewhat diplomatic trying to determine who killed the Lakota.

"The arrow did not come from our people. I want to see it to know it is a Cheyenne arrow."

Boots could tell a Cheyenne arrow as well. Migisi made his arrows in the Cheyenne custom.

One of the scouts from the back trail came to Harkahoma and whispered something to him. Boots heard Harkahoma order all the scouts to come to him.

"Find them all and bring them here."

It would be unfortunate for the trip to the Cheyenne village to be interrupted. Nokomis could pass away by the time they got there and that is something Boots did not want to happen.

When all the scouts were brought in, Harkahoma held up one hand to Boots to signify five of the braves were lost. This would not sit well with Chief Ehane, and they were not even halfway to the village.

Without warning, a hundred or so Lakota surrounded

the Cheyenne party. Harkahoma looked to find the one in charge. When he thought he located him, he started speaking.

"You have killed many braves. You must want war. If that is what you want, that is what you will get."

The leader of the Lakota band scoffed at Harkahoma's remarks.

"You who are surrounded by my people tell me you will bring war. I tell you that you will not be able to bring war. You belong to us."

The leader shouted instructions to the Lakota braves to close in tight around the Cheyenne and lead them to the Lakota village. Boots thought he recognized the leader of the band, and he understood the language. He knew Harkahoma did not speak Lakota. He turned to him to tell him his plans.

"Harkahoma, they want to take us to their village. I know this man and I know the chief. I will see if he will let you pass on while I go parlay."

Harkahoma simply nodded his approval. He did not appear to be pleased with Boots going alone.

Boots nudged his mustang in the direction of the leader.

"My name is Boots. We are on a journey to the Cheyenne village where Chief Ehane's wife lay near death. These brave men came to get me to go to the village. If you will let them pass, I will go with you to see Chief Enapay."

When he said the name of the chief, the Lakota leader made his mind up quickly.

"You speak my language. You come with me. The rest of you leave here now."

Boots told Harkahoma that he and his braves would be free to go. He asked that one of the scouts double back and let Trapper John know what has happened and for him to continue on to the village.

Once Boots separated from the Cheyenne, he began to feel uneasy. The Lakota leader needed to return to the village with a trophy and Boots hoped he could fill that bill, but he needed to stay alive. He thought his idea was too easily accepted by the Lakota leader. The words had barely left his mouth before the leader agreed.

Without turning and looking, Boots could feel Harkahoma following the band to the Lakota village. He rarely had second thoughts about something, but he had to try to figure out a way out of the mess he created. No straps were put on the captive as ordered by the leader. Boots thought it would make it easier to escape, but then that would solve nothing, but create another confrontation. He hoped he could make it to the Lakota village and talk with Chief Enapay. They did not stop to camp at night, instead, they continued to the village.

When they arrived, no drums were heard as in the Cheyenne village. The warriors went their separate ways as the leader took Boots to the lodge of Chief Enapay.

The leader of the war party reported their successes to the chief.

"We have taken Cheyenne life, and we have captured this man who claims his name to be Boots. He also thinks he knows you."

The war party leader snickered at his remark.

The Lakota chief looked angry. He told the leader to leave them. Boots saw that he recognized him.

"Why are you here? My warriors killed Cheyenne. Cheyenne killed my best hunter. This we know. Why did you come here?"

"You remember me, Chief Enapay. I am here to make sure there is no war. Your warriors took five of the Cheyenne. I hope it ends there, but I know the Cheyenne chief will be unhappy. Do you have the arrow that killed your hunter? If you do, I want to see it."

Chief Enapay sent a youth to his lodge to fetch the arrow. He returned with a broken arrow, the point was gone, but the chief handed the shaft of the weapon to Boots.

"My warrior said this is the arrow of the Cheyenne. I do not know."

"Chief, this arrow did not come from the bow of a Cheyenne. I have many arrows made by Cheyenne. These feathers are wrapped. The Cheyenne use tree sap to bind the feathers to the shaft. The shaft is too long and is the wrong wood."

"You know a lot about the Cheyenne arrows. It seems I have been told wrong. But, someone killed my best hunter and I must avenge his death. We have done so. I will send a message to the Cheyenne chief. We do not want war."

A pack full of gifts from Chief Enapay for Boots to give to Chief Ehane rested behind his saddle.

"I cannot make promises for Chief Ehane, but I will tell him what has happened."

Thankful he did not get drawn and quartered at the hands of the Lakota, Boots left the village and soon found Harkahoma and the remainder of his entourage. He told the old man what happened, but Harkahoma did not accept the explanation.

"His warriors killed my people. We will strike back."

Silence became the order of the day as the group headed for the Cheyenne village.

18

Trapper John, Trapper Bailer, and Whistler never got the message about the whereabouts of Boots. They continued to the Cheyenne village and found that he never arrived. After leaving his belongings with Migisi, the three men took off to find Boots.

"I know a mountain man such as Boots will not get lost on the mountain. Something happened to him and those braves that were with him."

Whistler started up with his tune.

"I want everybody to know that we are looking for Boots. I think he can hear my whistling from a long way off."

Having no idea where to search, the trio backtracked on their trail from the cave to the village. About halfway along, Trapper John called a halt. He motioned for Trapper Bailer over to join him. Bailer could track a fruit fly looking for fruit.

"There is a disturbance here and I think I see blood spots on the leaves."

"I believe a skirmish happened here, John. Everybody left in that direction."

Bailer pointed westward as he looked down at the ground.

"These are Indian ponies, and there are a bunch of them. They must have been surprised or something. I know Boots would put up a fight."

The Cheyenne following the Lakota disturbed the tracks of the leading bunch, but Bailer could tell a good number of people were on the trail. They continued to follow the tracks. Whistler told Trapper John that he knew of a Lakota tribe that could be found if they continued in the direction they were heading. Trapper John whispered to Whistler.

"There are scouts on either side of us right now. I can't tell if they are Lakota or Cheyenne."

Whistler finally spotted one of the scouts and whispered to Trapper John that he thought they were Cheyenne. He started whistling again and attracted the attention of the scouts. They watched the three men as they continued westward on the trail.

"I can hear one of my friends," Boots turned to Harkahoma who had a blank expression on his face. He nudged his mustang out in front.

Boots made a noise much like the stellar Jay would make.

"Boots has us. That is his call," Whistler urged his horse ahead.

After an hour, both parties came into visual contact with each other. Boots was unaware Trapper John never got the message about the Lakota.

"Stop. Something is wrong here."

Trapper John held up his hand to tell the other two mountain men to halt.

"I saw ten or so Cheyenne leave with Boots. There are a bunch of them missing."

Boots held both hands to his face and shouted to John.

"We are coming. Everything is fine. Stay where you are."

Boots nudged the mustang into a lope.

"I sure am glad to see you. We thought something bad happened."

"I am fine. The Lakota killed some of our Cheyenne because they thought the Cheyenne killed their hunter. A bunch of them swooped in on us. They took me and let Harkahoma go on, but he followed us instead. I see now you did not get my message to go on to the village."

"We went to the village, and your wife is of a fit because

you didn't come with us. We had no idea of what happened so we came looking."

"I talked with the Lakota chief and I saw the arrow that killed their hunter. It was not a Cheyenne arrow. Once I convinced him of that, he gave me gifts to give to Chief Ehane for the five braves they killed. Harkahoma is still not happy. I can tell he wants revenge. But, I think it will be up to the chief to decide. I am anxious to get to the village, so why don't we move on out."

When they arrived at the village, Harkahoma took the opportunity to report to Chief Ehane first. The chief sequestered himself in a lodge next to his to keep from disturbing Nokomis.

Boots heard loud talking when he approached the lodge. Two braves stood to watch over the door and they stopped Boots from entering.

"Chief, I need to talk with you. I have an important message from Chief Enapay."

Boots held the pack from the Lakota chief in his arms. No signal to enter came from in the lodge. He waited until Harkahoma came through the door. He gave Boots an angry look before he hurried away.

Boots waited a few more minutes before he heard the word come muttered.

When he entered the chief's lodge, Boots was surprised to see many of the elders sitting in a circle around the fire pit. They were waiting on the death word from the lodge next door.

"My brother who I trust with my life has told me the Lakota killed five of the men who went with him to bring you home. And, he tells me you talked with the Lakota chief and have sympathy for them. I must hear your story."

Boots continued to hold the pack as he started his story.

"A Lakota hunter was killed with an arrow they thought came from a Cheyenne. When the Lakota warriors found us, they fought. Our warriors battled with honor, but there were so many Lakota, we lost five. The leader closed in on us and we stood no chance to escape. Harkahoma tried to talk to the leader, but the leader does not know Cheyenne. I know Lakota so I talked to him. He agreed to take me to his chief and he let Harkahoma and his five warriors leave. They followed us to the Lakota village. I talked to Chief Enapay. I saw the arrow. It is not Cheyenne. When I showed him the difference he said he had been misinformed. He sent these gifts to the High Chief of the Cheyenne Ehane."

Boots handed the chief the pack. Stones fell out of the pack. When the chief picked them up, they glittered from the gold in the stone. He passed the stones to the elders. He found beads, and other trinkets, and finally, a feather from an eagle for Chief Ehane's headdress.

"You tell the story my brother tells, but a little differently. He did not go to the village. He does not know of this. He wants war. Your story tells me there will be no war."

The chief looked at each one of the elders sitting with their legs crossed. Each one nodded their head yes.

"The elders have spoken. They believe your story. There will be no war. And that is good because Nokomis is not well. My daughter Migisi has gone high on the rock to speak to the Great Spirit. He is waiting for the daughter of the moon to come to him. It will be a sad day and a day of celebration for the Great Spirit. You must go to Migisi."

Boots and Migisi spent little time catching up. Migisi told him she had finished grieving for her mother. She knew the time is near.

"Mother cannot talk. Her eyes are closed. She breathes very little. Her place is built, and I will wrap her in this red blanket. I know my mother is at peace already, and the spirits await her arrival."

Migisi went to be by her mother's side because she wanted to be with her when the time comes. Boots sought Red Feather, the son of Chief Ehane and Migisi's brother.

"The village is ready. Everyone will honor my mother, Nokomis. There is no one here to say a bad word about her. They all liked my mother. Many times she would help with the sick in almost every lodge. We celebrate her rising."

Boots became familiar with the traditions of the Cheyenne years ago when some warriors died in a battle. The place Migisi referred to would be on a scaffold in the air so Nokomis would be closer to the Great Spirit. She would be wrapped in that red blanket. And mourners would spend time at the site. Normally, the dead person's belongings would be handed out to close family or distributed among those in the village. However, being the chief's wife, her belongings would be given to Migisi.

19

The wailing started early in the morning. Nokomis had succumbed to death. Migisi woke Boots to let him know her mother died and she used the red blanket to wrap her body. Sons of the elders would carry the body to the scaffold built for her. Most of the village members followed behind Chief Ehane. Once she was placed on her final resting place, the women started cutting their hair as one of the traditions. Migisi wore her hair in a braid, and she used the big hunting knife from Boots' scabbard to cut from her head. The women stayed with the scaffolding even when Chief Ehane heard the ceremonial 'come back' drum. The 'come back' meant for the grieving family to return to the village so the members of the village could help them through their grief.

Migisi and Boots sat together. Across from them was Chief Ehane. Red Feather did not return for the 'come back' tradition. Migisi kept a watch on her father and she saw resilience in him she did not see before this day. He started talking of Nokomis.

"We were young together. We were together for many years. She knew me better than I know myself. I tried to know her, but she went to deep for me sometimes. I played my tapenho one night, and she came to me on that big rock. It was very dark and I learned then why she earned the name Nokomis. She was the daughter of the moon as her name says. I will remember her every day.

Those in the circle agreed with Chief Ehane. Stories were told and three songs were sung before the 'come back' tradition ended. When they reached their lodge, Migisi turned to Boots to speak.

"I am glad you are here. I am ready to leave. I want to go home now."

"We have two homes. One is the Whispering Pines Ranch, and the other is up in the mountain."

"That is where I want to be now. I want silence and peace. I want us to be together again."

Boots and Migisi spent very little time together while her mother lingered near death. To Boots it seemed like many months, but Migisi stayed for only two months. She started packing things she wanted to take with her to the cave. Her mother gave her a necklace that came from

Migisi's grandmother. It was very old, and a prized possession of Nokomis and now Migisi. She put the necklace on.

"This will help you protect us on our journey home."

Migisi and Boots shared a cup of coffee early the next morning. Chief Ehane stepped into the lodge.

"I know you are ready to leave my daughter. You gave your mother everything you could give. You will always remember her and you will always be my daughter. I hope to see you before you have to take care of me in the same way."

The chief laughed at his own comment.

"We will return Father. It will not be so long. I want to go to our home where I find peace again."

Chief Ehane bid his daughter goodbye and shook the offered hand of Boots before he left the lodge.

Boots and Migisi felt a release of stress when Chief Ehane left. The time now was their own.

Made in United States
North Haven, CT
17 June 2023

37905054R00078